HOMELESS
Man

HOMELESS *Man*

Malcolm Chester

HOMELESS MAN

This book is written to provide information and motivation to readers. Its purpose is not to render any type of psychological, legal, or professional advice of any kind. The content is the sole opinion and expression of the author, and not necessarily that of the publisher.

Printed in the United States of America.

ISBN   978-1-64552-129-7   (Paperback)
ISBN   978-1-64552-130-3   (Digital)

Lettra Press books may be ordered through booksellers or by contacting:

Lettra Press LLC
18601 Green Valley Ranch Blvd.
Unit 108, Box 204 Denver, CO 80249
1 303 586 1431 | info@lettrapress.com
www.lettrapress.com

PROLOGUE

The cold Chicago night cut through the young man inside the elaborate cardboard shelter. As a well-educated man, he understood the absence of heat very well. The young man carried so many layers of smelly clothing, he could barely move his arms and legs but the layers kept him relatively warm. This would be all he needed until the morning or at least so he thought.

The commotion started at the other end of the settlement where the drumfires began. Some of the toughs, part of one gang or another, beat up his fellow outcasts. The toughs needed to beat up someone who wouldn't fight back for a change to satisfy the rage that burned inside of them. When their arms grew tired and their fists sore, they would stop, long before they reached the young man. Tonight he would be safe. Two nights ago, he hadn't been so lucky. The young man still bore the bruises of that night.

The noise assaulting his ears suddenly changed. A shot rang out followed by several more shots. People screamed in terror and cursed loudly in both English and Spanish. His homeless brothers and sisters ran toward him. The toughs had found others of their kind. While they had inflicted pain, greater pain waited for them. Bullet wounds healed slowly and painfully and sometimes not at all. The young man actually felt sorry for his tormentors. Many of them would not see the dawn. The young man began to stir. He might need to run away. He peeked out of his shelter toward the noise but to his relief the shouts and curses began to move away. Still after tonight the young man must change his habits. He would need shelter in the nights ahead. Otherwise this senseless violence would claim him as it had so many others this night.

CHAPTER 1

The stunningly beautiful woman with violet eyes tapped her fingers on the well-worn breakfast table in a crowded noisy restaurant. She still felt the sweat on her soft skin from her morning work out at the East Bank club, the price she paid for keeping her beautiful figure. The woman's next stop would be the hot shower waiting at home for her. A steaming cup of coffee next to some partly eaten scrambled eggs stared at her as the old electric clock on the wall kept the time with a soft whir. As the woman began to wonder whether she should leave, an attractive blond woman seemingly out of nowhere slipped in the booth opposite her. She bounced in her seat as she started the conversation.

"Mary Ann, I'm sorry I'm late. Nine a.m. on a Saturday is very early for me. What could be so important that you would need to see me now."

"I've made a decision Tiffany that I want to share with you. I wanted to tell you now because I'll be busy the rest of the day and may forget."

"You could have called or e-mailed me but I admit talking in person is always better. Have you decided to get back together with Barry? I could never understand why you broke up with him in the first place. That man marked all the boxes."

"No, I'll never return to Barry."

"Because it makes no sense, one of these days you will have to tell me why. You know I will keep asking until you do. It drives me crazy not to know."

"Oh okay. I think I know now. At first, I didn't want to admit the reason. As perfect as Barry is, I couldn't see myself spending the rest of my life with him and having his babies. I didn't want to become the person I knew I would become. I'm looking for something different but what that is I haven't a clue."

"Then you should come out with me tonight and troll for men. With you along, men rush to our table. If I play my cards right, I can pick up one of the ones you discard."

"Come on Tiffany. Since when have you needed me or any other woman to help you attract men? Every time we meet there is another one. The last one was Rutger I think. Why aren't you going out with him?"

"He wrung some of the right chimes for me sexy and smart. I would have gone to bed with him, but he pushed me too hard. That is the one thing that always turns me off."

"It's the same way with me Tiffany. I have to tell a guy I'm ready before I'll have sex with him. Anyway I came to tell you something. So here it is. On Saturdays, I'm going to volunteer at a homeless center six blocks west of here. I did the same thing during college."

"Yuck, why would you want to do something like that? Half of the homeless are fresh out of a mental hospital. The smell bad and can be violent. It's really dangerous hanging around people like that. If you have to volunteer why don't you volunteer at a children's facility. They're cute and need you just as much."

"But they're not nearly as interesting. Homeless people are full of hard luck stories if you can persuade them to share. They're like hundreds of songs and novels walking around in their dirty clothes. You know I like to write songs and novels. I haven't written any in a while. I'm hoping this experience will help me get started. I have a serious case of writer's block."

"I'm not the creative type like you. I sell industrial equipment for a living. Which is why I need to go out tonight. I sold thirty forklifts this week. I can afford to buy some drinks if the guys aren't paying."

"I have never seen you buy a drink. You just flash those blue eyes of yours and the drinks appear."

"You should talk. All you need to do is walk into a room. Men just stare at you. You have three offers for a drink before you even sit down."

"Which is why I'm not going out trolling with you tonight. I don't feel like avoiding advances tonight. I think I have heard every line men can invent."

"It all depends on who is delivering the line. You know that. Okay, I guess you volunteering at a homeless center is a neat thing. It sure is different. Let me know what goes on there and remember my offer to go out tonight is still on the table. Now if you don't mind I have places to go and things to do."

"I'll walk out with you. I need a hot shower and to get ready for my first visit to the shelter."

"Well I guess someone in that place will smell good." Tiffany said as she walked to the door with Mary Ann beside her.

CHAPTER 2- THE HOMELESS CENTER

Mary Ann dressed down as well as she could with loose jeans and a matching denim shirt and her luxuriant brunette hair in a bun. The Homeless Center looked very much like the one she used to frequent in Boston. The large industrial kitchen, the cafeteria line and the cheap furniture occupying almost every square foot remaining already felt a little like home. Mary Ann walked right up to a middle age strong looking woman who seemed to be in charge. She spoke with her hand extended.

"I'm Mary Ann. I spoke to a woman named Susan about volunteering here on Saturdays. She said it was okay."

"I'm Roberta, a senior volunteer. Susan Beaumont is the Executive Director. She doesn't come in most Saturdays. If she says you're okay, you're okay with us. Grab an apron. We're making soup and hash, what we usually make. You can help chop vegetables, serve when we open and then clean up when we are done. Have you ever done this before?"

"As a mater of fact I have. I volunteered at a Homeless Center in Boston. This looks pretty much the same."

"I'm sure it is. By the way this is Terry, Bonnie and Kathy. They volunteer on Saturdays too. If you have questions or issues, any of us can help."

After Mary Ann introduced herself to the rest of the workers, she fell right into the work routine. At eleven, the patrons started filtering in for lunch. They seemed to appear from many different locations. The men and women varied tremendously in appearance and age. Many of them had the blank stare of the streets but others liked to engage in conversation. As Mary Ann ladled soup into their bowls, she watched and listened to them very carefully. She already started to hear parts of the stories she came to hear. Not all of what they said would be true but nonetheless she heard some interesting tidbits of life on the streets and the worlds from where some of them came. Many did not talk. Mary Ann would have to work harder to hear some of their stories. She expected they would be the most interesting.

One hot topic of conversation centered on the gang war that erupted at one of the homeless camps on the near west side. A gang of toughs in the process of beating up some homeless people suddenly found themselves under attack from a rival gang. Ten people died and fifteen people ended up in the hospital from the gunfire that erupted. Two homeless people were among the dead. After hearing various versions of the story, Mary Ann asked one of the talkative ones Bert, a hulking bearded man with a particularly foul odor, a question.

"How many of you were there?"

"None of us beautiful lady except Edward over there. He never says very much, but is the cleanest man or woman in the camps. He is one of us but at the same time he doesn't seem like one of us. Most of the day we don't see him. Then he shows up at a camp or here for a meal. He is a strange one but of course most of us are a little strange. If the government wasn't so cheap, many of us would be in mental institutions where we could get our meds, a warm bed and three square meals a day. Believe it or not, I used to teach high school until one day all my kids began to look like lizards. When I asked my students what kind of bugs they ate, the principal asked me to leave the school."

"Bert that is an interesting story but I think I like to hear what happened from someone who actually was there. Terry, can you take over soup duty for a while? I think we should learn first hand what happened the other night."

"Glad to Mary Ann. We need to know more about what happened. Edward usually doesn't talk but with your looks you may be able to persuade him to talk."

"Thanks Terry. I'll sure try."

Mary Ann removed her apron and walked boldly to the small table where Edward finished his hash and soup. Edward watched Mary Ann approach but didn't say anything. Mary Ann accustomed to men trying to engage her found herself talking first.

"Hi Edward, I'm Mary Ann. I just started to volunteer here. I heard from the others that you were at the shootout the other night. Everyone is talking about it but you were the only one there."

Edward stared at Mary Ann for several minutes and then said.

"What do you want to know?"

"What happened? The homeless community has a hard enough time without having to face gang violence."

"Violence is a natural outgrowth of our predator and protective instincts. Society is supposed to help us control these instincts but for those who don't respect government or law violence is the result. Society does not protect homeless people so they are natural victims of its violent citizens. What happened two nights ago has happened before and will happen again. The details aren't terribly important. There doesn't have to be a good reason. On the outskirts of society any reason will do."

"I agree with you but I still would like to hear the details. If you can't remember, just tell me what you can."

"I remember everything. I have a photographic memory. The Power Rangers Crew claim the homeless camp as part of their turf. Since they feel it is their right to collect from every business and person in their area, they punish those of us in the community who do not pay. No free passes as they often say. We have no money so they routinely come by and punish us for not paying. Because they sometimes find items of value among us that we brought from another life or found, they will take these items and reduce the amount of punishment we receive. Two nights ago, they found nothing of value among us so they started beating up the people nearest to them.

"Then quite suddenly, a rival gang, the Black Swords, showed. They told the Power Rangers Crew and anyone else that would listen about a month ago that they were taking over part of the Power Ranger Crew's territory, which includes the homeless camp. The Power Ranger Crew's refused to cede their territory then or when confronted the other night. So the Black Swords attacked them with guns blazing two nights ago. The Power Ranger Crew fought back. Homeless people, Black Swords and Power Ranger Crew died and were injured in the shootout but when police sirens could be heard in the distance, the gangs both left without resolving the conflict. The Power Ranger Crew and the Black Swords will continue to fight until one side wins and the other side loses. Then the homeless camp will have the same masters and the same rules or different masters with the same rules. For us, nothing will change.

"I heard the fight from my card board house on the other end of the camp. I didn't go toward the fight or run away. I stayed in my little house. I didn't want to become a target. So I can't identify who did the shooting, nor would I want to do so. Homeless witnesses, who more often than not lack credibility in court, are frequently killed. Even if I were believed in court, why would I want to put a gang member away in prison when a new one will take his place? He and his friends would hate me and seek to take revenge on me for rating them out to the police. To survive on the streets, one has to play by the rules of the street."

"What you say makes a lot of sense. I can see why you acted the way you did. I have a lot to learn about your world. But you are not like the other people around here. You wear clean clothes. You are rational and sound quite intelligent. You show no signs of mental illness or of using drugs. Why are you here?"

"This center has the best free food in town. You ladies do a nice job."

"That's not what I meant and you know it." Mary Ann said a little too sharply.

"I shouldn't really respond to you when you talk like that, but the answer is a simple one. I'm living off the grid because this is the only place I can live, be free and relatively safe. Now I must really go. On Saturday afternoons, I visit the Public Library and read their excellent collection of ancient texts. The librarian and I like to debate various subjects raised in the books. Today we are discussing the amount of communication between ancient Egypt and Mesopotamia. I think there is evidence of a great deal, but my librarian friend does not believe the evidence."

"How can your cardboard box home be safe in the middle of a gang war?"

"It isn't. So, I found some very modest lodgings instead. I will be safer there. Now I must really go Mary Ann. I hope we have a chance to talk again."

"So do I. Enjoy your discussion." Mary said as she waived at the departing Edward. Mary Ann returned to food line with a very puzzled look on her face.

THE CHICAGO PUBLIC LIBRARY

Mary Ann as usual spent a good part of Sunday preparing for her next week at the trendy public relations firm where she worked. Mary Ann did a variety of things at the firm from working on annual corporate reports to developing slogans for advertising and marketing campaigns. She particularly excelled at developing catchy slogans, which delighted her bosses and customers alike. Mary Ann, however, only worked on this job because she had to do so. Her true love lay in journalism and music. In school, she worked on the school newspaper and then as an investigative journalist for a small city newspaper when she graduated with a journalism degree. Slowly though her dreams began to fade as newspaper and magazine after newspaper and magazine began to fold, including the one where she worked. Eventually, she arrived in Chicago and found a new home in the Hawthorne Public Relations Agency.

The investigative part of her did not die, however, and as a result, she became intrigued, even obsessed with Edward the homeless man she just met: a homeless man who wasn't really a homeless man who had a photographic memory and debated ancient history with a librarian. Where did he come from? Why was he on the streets? What talents did he possess? She had to find out.

So in a radical departure from her usual routine, Mary Ann on Tuesday rushed out of her agency at lunchtime and took a cab to the Chicago Public Library. Without a moment's hesitation, Mary Ann took the elevator to the third floor, where a librarian named Rachel waited for her. As a skilled reporter, Mary Ann knew she would obtain much more information from Rachel in person than she would on the phone. Mary Ann found out on line, the woman who ran the ancient history department and had called and made an appointment to see her. Mary Ann smiled as she approached the rather severe looking middle-aged woman.

"Hi I am Mary Ann. You're probably wondering why I'm here. I didn't really tell you on the phone. I volunteer at a Homeless Pantry. This past Saturday I ran into a man named Edward who claimed he debated ancient history with you. Although Homeless people can be difficult to speak with, we try to gather what information we can on them so we can help them if they are lost or in trouble. I'm just following up on his claim. Sometimes, these people can invent things which aren't really true."

"I see why you are interested in Edward. He showed up here about a year ago. He had some bandages on his face. Edward claimed he had an accident but the scars looked more like plastic surgery scars to me. I know about them. I had a little work done myself. Anyway, he told me he had an interest in ancient history and heard that I had a collection of ancient books that didn't appear anywhere on line. I said I did and pointed them out to him. With little more being said, he began to read the texts every Saturday at the same time. Within a month, he had read everything there and continued to read more works on line. This surprised me, as many of the books were written in Latin, Greek, or even the Aramic languages. I asked him about it and he shrugged his shoulders and said that he translated them. After he read the collection, Edward and I began to debate ancient history. Edward had a particular interest in ancient science, claiming that the ancients knew more science than we think."

"He sounds pretty smart."

"Yes, but it goes beyond that. I think Edward is a genius. About two months ago, I had to go to the main floor for a meeting and I passed by the computer cubicles. Edward sat there like a concert pianist in the most isolated cubicle. His hands literally flew across the keyboard. I positioned myself so I could see what he typed. I could barely believe my eyes. Complex math formulas interspaced with strange numbers that looked like spatial coordinates covered the screen and disappeared from the screen as new formulas and coordinates appeared. I studied math in college and recognized some of the symbols but what appeared on that screen soared far beyond my comprehension. I have no idea what problems those numbers solved but they appeared to somehow work toward a solution. I eventually tore myself away from his screen and hurriedly walked to my meeting. I don't know to this day whether he knew I watched him or not. If he did, Edward made no mention of it in our subsequent meetings."

"Wow. Edward is even more fascinating that I thought. Do you have any other information on him?"

"No not really but I think he likes music. He mentioned once how much he likes violin music."

"Does he play? I actually played as a child but I can't say I was very good. I am a much better singer than a player of musical instruments. I used to sing at bars and other public places."

"Yeah. I play the cello much to the chagrin of my neighbors. I can carry some basic tunes but if I try to go beyond that it sounds pretty scratchy. I sing too in my church's choir. As to Edward, he never mentioned whether he played or not but somehow I think he does."

"I sounded pretty scratchy too. Listen Rachel I have to go. You have been extremely helpful. I think all of us need to watch out for Edward. He may have something valuable to contribute to society. We don't want him to be hurt or badly injured on the streets."

"That's my concern as well and is why I told you all these things about him. Even though he has been out there for awhile, I don't think Edward appreciates how dangerous Chicago streets can be."

THE NEXT SATURDAY

The moment she entered the Homeless Pantry Mary Ann began to work. Roberta quickly approached her.

"Mary Ann I don't know how you did it but you persuaded our most taciturn client to speak last week. What did he say?"

"That he intended to meet a librarian at the Chicago Public Library and discuss ancient history. As a one-time journalist, I followed up and talked to the librarian. She thinks Edward is a genius. He read her ancient texts in their original language and she saw him writing some very advanced mathematical calculations on a computer in the library."

"That doesn't surprise me at all. I'm a senior partner in a major LaSalle Street Law Firm and know what smart people look like. I pegged Edward as one of those people from the start."

"Roberta, with your big job what are you doing here?"

"I help one rich guy or company take money from another rich guy or company. It is very lucrative but provides me with no personal satisfaction. This gig does, especially when it turns up lost geniuses."

"I understand that. I guess that is why I'm here too. My girlfriends think I ought to be out hunting boys but I'm here instead."

"I doubt you need to hunt boys. I'm sure they come to you. Anyway, you can do this and still date boys."

"Yeah I know, but I don't like too many things going on in my life. Very few boys will understand what I'm doing here. I don't want to start having fights over how I spend my time. I already had this experience and don't want to repeat it."

"I understand that. My husband hates that I come here. He wants me to concentrate on cooking one of my great meals on Saturday. I don't have time to do that if I come here."

"Yes this sounds just like a guy. Well I guess we need to set up this lunch line. The clients will be coming through that door very soon. Nice talking to you Roberta." Mary Ann said as she suddenly walked away.

Edward came very late in the lunch period. Mary Ann began to worry that he wouldn't show up. She had uncovered part of his story, but she needed to find out the whole story. Mary Ann smiled at Edward as she filled his plate with hash. Edward smiled at Mary Ann and simply said thank you. After he sat and ate for a while, Mary Ann approached him as before.

"Edward I thought you would seek me out, but you sit here as before. I'm not used to having to start conversations."

"Mary Ann I'm not used to talking with beautiful women. They've never given me the time of day before. They usually throw a few nasty words at me with the word Geek somewhere in the mix. I guess it is socially acceptable to talk to a poor downtrodden homeless man, but if I were a normal man with a job I think you would use the same words as those other women. "

"That's not very fair. I'm not a type. I don't go out with a man just because he is good looking. Anyway, you're pretty good looking for a man that lives on the street."

"Thanks for the compliment. Since you want to speak with me, I must have made you curious with my comments about ancient history."

"Well yes you did. I did a little checking. I used to be an investigative journalist. You not only read ancient history but you do so in several ancient languages. What's more, you speed-write advanced mathematical equations. That is pretty impressive."

"I see you have been speaking to Rachel. As to the foreign languages, it is simply a matter of using a dictionary. I read very fast so it seems like I know the languages. As to the mathematical equations, they're a hobby. I trade calculations with other math geeks like myself. It is pretty boring stuff for most people but I enjoy doing it."

"You have advanced degrees?"

"Yes many of them."

"I don't suppose you will tell me where you got them and what they are in."

"No I won't. What would be the fun in that? You will have to work a little harder on my story than that. I'll tell you what. If you want to know what I really like to do spend a few hours with me after lunch next week and I will show you."

"Are you asking me on a date? I don't usually go out with a man unless he asks me eight times. This is only once and you are a homeless man after all."

"It isn't a date but merely you finishing a story. If you want me to ask you out seven more times right now I can do that."

"Very funny. Okay as long as this is part of a story, I'll go with you for a few hours but under no circumstances can this be considered a date."

"I wouldn't think of embarrassing you that way. Anyway, I have to run. The mysteries of the ancient world await me."

Mary Ann watched Edward leave with anger twisting her beautiful face. A homeless man had calmly exposed her most hated flaws. Although she would never admit it to herself, Mary Ann always dated the man or boy with the highest status in her world. She would never accept anything less. She called it checking the boxes. Yet, she would do things like volunteer for a Homeless Pantry, knowing full well that the men she dated wouldn't understand it or do what she did. Worst of all, she had just measured this homeless man like any other man.

A man Tim very much like her now ex fiancée Barry had been pursuing her for months every Saturday morning at the East Bank Club. Very good looking, athletic and a very successful investment banker, he checked all her boxes and then some. Although she had no plans to do so, when Tim asked her out for the eighth time this morning, she said yes without really considering the consequences. In a panic, Mary Ann persuaded Tiffany to ask out an old boyfriend. She wanted someone close by in case things didn't work out very well on this date. Just before

Mary Ann arrived at the pantry, Tiffany said an old flame Steve had agreed to go on a double date with the two of them and Tim who they did not know. Mary Ann e-mailed Tim and told him that Steve and Tiffany would be joining them. Tim responded with a simple okay.

While she should be very excited to be dating a handsome man, old romance movies had become just that old, Mary Ann felt very nervous. This is why she made the independence statements to Roberta earlier. She would have been okay if Edward hadn't exposed what she really planned on doing tonight. If she intended to date another Barry she might as well go back to him. Mary Ann had a lot invested in that relationship and knew what she would get. She had no idea what kind of man Tim would turn out to be. Mary Ann sighed and went back to work. Maybe all of this would make some sense after tonight but somehow she doubted it.

THE DATE

At first the date went very well. All four of them had a great deal of experience in this kind of setting and handled the situation as well as any late twenty something men and women could. They made jokes, laughed at the right time, told half way interesting stories, and enjoyed eating and drinking the excellent food and wine at the restaurant Tim picked. Then seemingly out of nowhere the little voice in Mary Ann's head began to sound warnings. She hadn't heard this voice in a very long time.

Mary Ann had difficulty explaining the voice to anyone else. It sounded when something threatened her but the voice rarely if ever explained why she should be threatened or by whom. The voice didn't even get it right every time. Still, most of the time the voice, which must be her unconscious mind, did sense something. With a sudden look of concern on her face, Mary Ann signaled Tiffany and excused herself to go to the restroom. Tiffany followed her inside.

"Okay Mary Ann what is going on? It isn't that crazy voice of yours is it?"

"Unfortunately, yes it is, but I can't figure out why. Tim hasn't done anything to trigger it. Sure he looks at me with desire in his eyes. If he didn't, I'd think I was losing my mo jo. He is supposed to look at me that way."

"Mary Ann sometimes I think you're crazy. Half the young women I know including me would be parading in front of this guy in our skimpiest bikini just to get this gorgeous guy's attention. He is even better looking and more successful than Barry and that is saying a lot.

I don't think I ever told you but I tried to hook up with Barry after you dumped him but he wouldn't have anything to do with me. I reminded him too much of you."

"Tiffany, Barry would have been a good guy for you, certainly better than any of the other guys you've dated. But he is gone from both of our lives. Help me out here. Tell me that being with Tim is okay."

"Of course it is. If it makes you feel any better, just kiss the guy goodnight and save the rest of it for a future date. Maybe then the voice will go away. But I can tell you this. I don't think I could stop just kissing that guy. I'd want a piece of him."

"Thanks Tiffany. That is what I needed to hear. I'll give him a kiss good night and wait for the fireworks to come at a later time. Now let's go and enjoy the rest of the dinner."

The dinner ended well. The four of them split up, Tim driving Mary Ann home in his Porsche when she asked him to do so. They had a pleasant conversation on the way back to her condo, but Tim refused to let Mary Ann off at the front door of her condo building. Instead, he found a parking place nearby and exited the car with her. The little voice returned. Mary Ann began to feel nervous, but allowed Tim to put his arm around her on the way to the condo. When she opened the door to the condo and turned to say goodnight, Tim pushed his way inside. Mary Ann objected but not as loudly as she should have.

Mary Ann waved to Randolph the powerful black man and ex golden gloves boxer behind the condo desk. Mary Ann always stopped to say hello to Randolph. They always had kind words for each other. Randolph allowed the couple to pass but watched them carefully.

Mary Ann's internal voice screamed but she seemed powerless to stop what took place. Finally, when Tim pushed the up button on the elevator, Mary Ann managed to say.

"Tim it's been a great evening, but I'm tired and need to get some sleep. I have a lot of work to do tomorrow. So let's say goodbye here."

Tim didn't respond. He merely shoved Mary Ann into the elevator and pushed the button for the fifth floor.

Not knowing what to do. Mary Ann said.

"How did you know what floor I lived on?"

"I saw your keys in your purse. The number 520 was easy to read."

Mary Ann didn't need her little voice anymore. Mary Ann allowed herself to be forced into a bad situation. She felt a strong attraction for Tim and had so far only offered very weak resistance. This would have to change. She would never allow herself to be pushed around this way.

When the elevator opened, Mary Ann resisted moving toward her door. Her voice took on a hard edge.

"That's enough. I'm going to my condo and you're leaving here at once. Our date is over. Now get your hands off of me."

Tim ripped Mary Ann's purse out of her hands and retrieved the key. Then he began to drag her toward her own door. Mary Ann now furious kicked Tim as hard as she could. Rage filled Tim's eyes. He punched Mary Ann in the stomach and as she doubled over in pain began to rip her cloths off in the hall.

"You damn bitch. I'll take you here in front of the whole floor." Tim screamed. Fighting the larger and stronger Tim as best she could, Mary Ann heard the elevator door open. Seconds later, Tim suddenly moved away from her and up against the wall. Randolph had a powerful grip on him and moved the two hundred pound Tim with ease.

Tim rummaged in his pocket and withdrew a pearl handled switchblade from his pants.

Mary Ann yelled. "Randolph, look out."

Randolph saw the switchblade and ripped it out of Tim's hand. Then he followed that action up with a flurry of punches to Tim's stomach and jaw. With a final powerful right hook, he sent Tim crashing to the floor. Tim didn't move. Blood trickled out of his nose. Randolph turned to Mary Ann.

"Are you alright? Something didn't seem right to me about this guy. So I followed both of you on the cameras in the elevator and the floor. As soon as he started dragging you I headed for the elevators. I'm glad I got here in time. He was seconds away from violently raping you."

"Yeah you have that right. I can't thank you enough, Randolph. I'm shaking so badly, it's going to take me a few minutes to pull myself together. I think I 'm in shock."

"Do you want to go to the hospital or the police? I may haul him down there myself. He pulled a knife on me."

"Do what you want to him. I don't care, but I don't need a hospital and I can't handle a police station. Even though he intended to, he never really raped me. I just need to crawl into bed and forget this ever happened. But answer me one question. Why did you help me? You could have gotten yourself in a tricky situation. I didn't ask for your help, but as it turned out I sure needed it."

"Mary Ann you always stop and talk to me as a friend and an equal. You remember my birthday and my kid's birthdays. You always brighten my day. I would never let anything bad happen to you."

"Thanks for that Randolph. I might owe you my life. Now get that piece of trash out of here. I need to go to sleep."

"I'm happy to oblige."

After Mary Ann retrieved her keys from a knocked out Tim, she opened the door slowly, closed it and then began to cry. Mary Ann literally cried herself to sleep.

THE FOLLOWING WEEK

ary Ann's life slowly returned to normal. Randolph told Mary Ann that he had a serious conversation with Tim when he woke. Randolph told Tim that if he ever threatened Mary Ann again, he would take the hall and elevator video to the police. Tim promised to stay away and claimed that he had too much to drink and lost control.

To put the ugly incident out of her mind, Mary Ann concentrated on her work. When Tiffany asked her what happened, Mary Ann merely said that Tim and she wouldn't work out. She provided her friend with no details. Other than a bad bruise on her stomach, Mary Ann had no other physical injuries. When she took off for the Homeless Pantry on the next Saturday, Mary Ann had no idea whether she would spend several hours with Edward as she had promised.

Mary Ann approached Edward cautiously at the end of the pantry lunch. Her time with Tim still plagued her. Yet, her rational mind told her that Edward and Tim had no similarities. Unless she had completely lost her ability to judge people, Edward didn't attack women out of some sense of his masculine superiority. He wasn't the type.

"Hi Edward. I had a very tough week. I can spare a few hours but that is about it."

"That is all the time I need for what I want to show you. Remember this is not a date but me showing you a little about myself to satisfy your curiosity."

"Okay I'm ready. I began work early. It isn't my turn to do the dishes and clean up. "

"Then it is to our chariot we go. After all the CTA bus has a driver and it is taking us to where we want to go."

"I never thought of a CTA bus that way. Rather they look like road warrior vehicles with all the dings in their sides and the smashed bumpers."

"For today, it will be our chariot."

"Okay where are we headed?"

"To DePaul on state; then the little park across the street, near the Public Library."

"Sounds romantic. "

"It will be."

They boarded a few buses and soon found themselves in front of the downtown branch of De Paul. The conversation felt easy and non-threatening to Mary Ann. She finally began to relax. When they stepped off the bus, Edward said.

"I have to borrow something from the school. Then we'll go to the park."

"Okay." Mary Ann replied.

Edward took an elevator in the school lobby to the 4th floor and took a key out of his pocket. He opened a closet door and retrieved a violin case. He turned to Mary Ann.

"Okay now we will go to the park. I know a little place where I can play for you that shouldn't be too noisy."

"You're going to play for me. How sweet. I played violin a little as a child and sang in a number of small bands until it became clear I would never have a music career. Still I love music."

"I hope you like my playing. This is what I really like to do."

Edward found his little space in the small park. Despite it being a busy area, no one stood in this location. Edward hurriedly removed the beautiful violin. Tuned it a little. Then turned to Mary Ann and said.

"Well here we go."

What happened next astounded Mary Ann? She had no idea a violin could sound this good. The first pieces Edward played sounded like Chopin but Chopin didn't write for the violin. Mary Ann lost herself in the incredible sounds. They seemed to come from everywhere at once. Every note seemed perfect and blended flawlessly with the next. Then when she seemed to float away with the music, Edward suddenly changed to Beethoven playing one of his violin concertos. His bow and hands moved so quickly they looked like a blur. The music moved in a crescendo to the sublime. Then the music suddenly stopped, even though Mary Ann desperately wished for it to continue. Edward looked at Mary Ann expectantly as a small crowd that gathered clapped.

"Well what do you think? I have been adapting a few of Chopin's piano pieces to the violin. I like playing the piano almost as much as I do the violin."

"Edward you're an incredible violinist. You deserve to be a soloist with the Chicago Symphony or any other symphony in the world. I never knew a violin could sound like that." Mary Ann gushed.

"Thanks. Coming from you that means something to me. Most of the time I play for myself, but every once in a while I will play for others. I played for Professor Reynolds and he offered to lend me his violin. The professor thinks I am the best violinist he has ever heard. He wants me to play for the Chicago Symphony where he plays. I don't think I could ever do that but I appreciated him saying it."

"Edward why are you a Homeless person? With your talent, you could have a job tomorrow. I just don't understand."

"That is part of the mystery about me. I'm not going to just tell you. You'll just to have to find out on your own. I don't suppose you would like to take a walk with me. I'll take the violin back and we can go. I don't really feel like studying ancient history."

"No, I'm sorry Edward. I really have to be going. As I said earlier, I had a very hard time this week and need some time to myself. Thank you for sharing your music with me. I'll see you at the Homeless Pantry next Saturday."

"Okay, but I'll give you fair warning. I may ask you to do something like this again."

"If it is anything like today, I'll look forward to it." Mary Ann said. As she walked away, she saw Edward take the violin back to De Paul.

Almost at the bus stop, Mary Ann nearly ran into a middle-aged man who eyed her carefully.

"Excuse me, did Edward just play for you?"

"Yes, he did. Who might you be?"

"Professor Reynolds. He played my violin, but in a way I have never been able to play. I may want to enlist your help."

"How can I help?"

"He apparently likes you. I can see why. You're a very beautiful woman. Maybe you can help me persuade Edward to play at the Chicago Symphony. He always says no to me."

"I suppose I can try. We are not dating but we do talk at the Homeless Pantry every Saturday."

"Please try. In my thirty years of teaching I have never met a talent like his."

"It seems a little strange. I never thought I would be trying to persuade a homeless man to play at a symphony."

"Whatever Edward is and I expect he is much more than he is letting on, Edward is not a Homeless Man. He is simply the greatest violinist in the world."

Mary Ann took the bus home but barely noticed the trip and some men who desperately tried to gain her attention. Edward dominated her thoughts. As she walked into her condo and said hello to her friend Randolph, Mary Ann suddenly realized that she would much rather be walking with Edward than going up to her condo. What a strange thought.

ANOTHER PIECE OF THE PUZZLE

On Thursday, Mary Ann sat in her dentist's office at 5:30 pm waiting for her annual checkup and cleaning. She took excellent care of her teeth. On the table next to her sat a copy of Discover Magazine, a science magazine for normal people. An article, "World's greatest mind disappears" caught her attention. She quickly turned to the article and began to read it.

The article recounted the life of a young man named Isaac, who had the highest IQ ever recorded. Not surprisingly, he graduated with a PHD in math at MIT followed by another PHD from nearby Harvard in Astrophysics by the age of 22. He then proceeded to develop 100 patents for a wide variety of products that left him a wealthy man by the age of 24. While doing this, he obtained a medical degree on line. He didn't have time to attend classes so he studied for the degree on line. The US government then recruited Isaac to work in its research laboratories and by age 26 he reportedly developed a hyperspace projector that could move living and nonliving matter through wormholes to the various planets and moons in the solar system. To make the hyperspace projector work, he developed a new three-dimensional math system and a quantum computer, which made our best supercomputers look like a Ford Model T. This information came from a fired worker at the research laboratory where the projector resides.

The US government called the idea of a hyperspace projector science fiction nonsense, but had refused to explain what took place at the large Chicago area research facility with the massive energy infrastructure, the old Fermilab facility, where the machine reportedly resides. At age

28, Isaac reportedly developed a new advanced laser, which all the US armed services deployed on many of their weapon systems. Once again, the US armed services denied the creation of such weapons. According to the same source at Fermilab, this laser could take out an entire squadron of enemy fighters before they came in range of a single laser equipped US fighter or if mounted on a naval ship sink an aircraft carrier with one pulse.

Then quite suddenly, Isaac vanished without an explanation about a year ago. The scientists at the research facility know he is still alive as he regularly adjusts the programming on the hyperspace projector from a remote computer terminal but Isaac otherwise refuses to communicate with anyone. Although the government has initiated a massive search for Isaac, efforts to locate Isaac have so far been futile. His computer programming skills are so advanced that government programmers' attempts to trace his communication with the research facilities' computers have been unsuccessful. Another way the authorities are attempting to find Isaac is by carefully looking through any articles or other information about concert violinists. Isaac apparently can play at the maestro level and has always maintained that he would just like to play music and forget about the rest of his talents. The military, which denies Isaac has developed advanced weapons for it, nonetheless states that it is a serious security risk to the US for Isaac to be out there subject to kidnapping or intimidation by a foreign power. At the end of the article, a picture of a smiling 24-year old Isaac appeared.

Mary Ann stared intently at the picture. The face differed from the Edward she knew but the height weight and posture seemed identical. She folded the magazine and followed the nurse into the inner office. Ten minutes later, as the dental hygienist worked away, Mary Ann suddenly remembered what Rachel said about the bandages. Edward could very well be Isaac with a little plastic surgery to alter his appearance but she would wait before sharing her suspicions with anyone. She wanted to spend time with Edward on Saturday.

A GLORIOUS DAY

Saturday turned out to be a wonderful sunny warm day. Mary Ann didn't see Tim at the East Bank Club and as before began working at the Homeless Pantry very early. By the time Edward arrived and ate his lunch, Mary Ann already approached him. Edward just sat there looking at her with his shy sweet smile. He spoke first.

"Our chariot awaits. Will you spend time with me today? I just want to walk in our beautiful downtown and along the lake. Also, I want to briefly visit Blues Fest. Slim Walker is an old friend and he is playing."

"Sounds great. Let's go."

With that simple statement, they left together oblivious to anyone at the center. They talked of their love of music. When he played and she sang, they both felt at peace with the world. They spoke a little of their childhood. Both of them grew up in the Chicago area, even though Edward spent many years in the east. They observed everything around them from the patrons on the bus to the people walking on the streets. They commented on all of them. They walked downtown for a while and ended up at the Blues Fest. Edward led Mary Ann to the place Slim Walker played.

Slim Walker played his guitar and sang as if he sat on his sharecropper porch in Southern Mississippi. His guitar perfectly reflected his gravel-toned voice so at times they seemed like the same instrument. His wrinkled skin spoke of the hours he worked and sat in the strong Southern sun. Slim came from a long line of African American singers who created both the jazz and blues that served as the foundation of the pop and rock music of today. A group of devoted followers gathered around Slim, drinking in his wonderful music.

Slim looked down at Edward and smiled. When he came to the end of Catfish Blues, he paused and said in his gravely voice.

"Edward come on up here and play a little. Edward is the only white boy I ever met who really understands what blues is all about. He feels the pain, sorrow and heat of the South like I do. "

As Edward jumped on stage and picked up an extra Gibson Slim had on the stage, he merely smiled at the audience, put the guitar strap over his head and began to play. Once again, Mary Ann stood there in amazement. He played like Slim but with even more feeling punctuated by blistering fast runs. With his eyes closed and his head pointed upward, he completed a particularly fast run and just stopped.

The crowd clapped loudly but Edward paid them little attention. Instead Edward waved Mary Ann on stage and said.

"Is there a song you would like to sing?" Edward said.

"I don't know too many blues tunes but I used to sing Sweet Home Chicago at some of my gigs. Why don't we do that?"

"Great. Just what we need now. I'll start off playing and then you sing. Edward you join in as you see fit." Slim said answering Mary Ann.

Mary Ann started singing and a big smile came to her face. She found the soul in her voice and delighted at the wonderful accompaniment she received. The crowd began to sing with her. The moment seemed like magic. Mary Ann forgot how much she loved singing. All too soon the song ended. The crowd loved it. After Edward and Mary Ann bowed to the crowd and shook Slim's hand, Mary Ann and Edward quietly left the stage and waved goodbye to the crowd and their friend. Many in the crowd wondered who these very talented unknown people might be.

The couple remained at the Blues Fest for another hour. Edward introduced each act to Mary Ann and explained how they fit into the blues world. When they tired of the fest, they walked to the lake and turned north along the bike path. They walked and talked. The time just slipped away. They sang with a man along the path, performing for money. Edward left him a little change. Mary Ann didn't ask him from where it came, but she felt a little odd when a homeless man gave another man on the street money. When they became hungry, they snacked on a little food at the Lincoln Park Zoo. Before either of them realized it, the sun began to set as the time reached 7:30 pm. Mary Ann's condo lay just North of the zoo in Lakeview. Without really planning it, they found themselves there. Mary Ann spoke quickly.

"Edward I had a lovely time but I think I'll call it a night. It's getting dark and I don't want to walk any more."

"Fine: I had a fantastic time too. Mary Ann I'm going to say something, which may upset you but I feel that I have to say it. I love you. I don't really know why but I do. I have been attracted to other women but I have never really loved a girl before. These emotions are new to me. It is upsetting the plans I have but frankly I don't care. If you don't feel the same way, I completely understand. As a rule, girls don't like or understand me. With that I will bid you goodnight. I hope to see you at the pantry next week."

With that statement, Edward bent down and kissed Mary Ann lightly on the lips and turned on his heels and headed into the night.

Too stunned to react, Mary Ann watched Edward walk away. Just before he left her sight Mary Ann yelled after him.

"Isaac, I like you too and hope to see you next Saturday."

An hour later, Mary Ann paced in her apartment. To her great surprise, Mary Ann really liked Edward's kiss. In fact, she wanted to be kissing him right now. Edward differed greatly from any other boy she had ever been attracted to, but she felt the attraction nonetheless. Mary Ann reacted far too coldly to Edward's shy advances. Calling him Isaac also bothered her. Mary Ann said it to brag about her solving the puzzle of Edward's identity but she did so with little regard for Edward's privacy or situation. Obviously, for some good reason, he didn't want to work for the government any longer. So he became a homeless person to hide from them: a brilliant ploy from a brilliant man. Mary Ann feared he would avoid her now. If he did, she had no way to contact Edward. The next seven days would be anxious ones unless she somehow saw Edward sooner.

THE ANXIOUS WEEK

Mary Ann called Rachel at the library everyday asking whether she had seen Edward but each day she answered no. She also called his friend the music professor but he hadn't seen Edward either. Mary Ann grew more anxious as the week passed. Her utterance of a single word might have sent him away from all of them and perhaps even the area.

As usual, Mary Ann arrived at the Homeless Pantry early. She immediately began preparations. Soon the familiar volunteer crew joined her. At 10:50 am ten minutes before they began serving, a man looking very much like a detective walked into the facility. He approached Roberta who appeared to be in charge and extended his hand.

"Hi I'm private detective Rich Richardson. I have been hired by the FBI to help locate a very important scientist who has gone missing. I used to be a CPD detective and worked cases in this area. I wondered whether you might have seen this man. Posing as a homeless man would be a very good way for this scientist to hide."

As Rich spoke he handed Roberta a picture of a younger Isaac. Roberta passed the picture to all of the volunteers working at the center. Each person looked at the picture and shook their head. Finally, Roberta responded after all the workers at the pantry including Mary Ann shook their heads.

"I'm sorry, detective. We don't get many important scientists at this place. We receive the mentally ill, the chronically unemployed and others who have run out of luck. Each of us would have noticed someone like this. He would have stood out from our normal clients."

"Okay here is my card. When does your lunch service start?"

"It starts at 11 and ends at 2."

Roberta replied without hesitation.

"I hope you don't mind if I stick around."

"No just don't eat the food. It is for the homeless not working people like us."

"Not a problem, I have a sandwich in my car."

When Rich left, presumably to eat his sandwich, Robert turned quickly to Mary Ann.

"Can you contact Edward?"

"No but I have an idea of how I might intercept him. He walks through the door at around 1:28 every Saturday. The bus stop is five minutes away, which means his bus arrives at 1:23. I can check the schedule on my I-phone and board the stop before this one. Then I can ride with him to downtown passing this place. The detective didn't come here by accident. He already knows Edward eats lunch here on Saturdays. Someone must have told him."

"Leave now and don't come back until next week. Use the back door so the detective doesn't see you. If Edward is this Isaac, he needs our protection. It could be why he is homeless in the first place."

"Okay. If he asks where I went, say I went home sick."

At 1:23 Mary Ann boarded the bus at the stop before the one near the pantry. Edward sat in the back of the bus looking out the window. Mary Ann walked to the back of the bus and stood in front of him. She said.

"Edward we have to talk. Instead of going to the pantry we need to go downtown."

Edward smiled broadly at Mary Ann and said.

"Mary Ann it's great to see you. I'll go anywhere with you. We'll catch some lunch downtown instead."

Mary Ann and Edward avoided saying very much until they left the bus at Michigan and Illinois. They climbed the stairs to North Michigan Avenue and started walking. Edward began:

"Why did you get on my bus like that?"

"A detective looked for a man named Isaac at the center. If you had left the bus at your regular stop he would have seen you."

"Who is Isaac? You mentioned his name the other night?"

"You or at least it used to be you."

After pausing for several minutes, Edward finally said. "Oh, what tipped you off?"

"A talk with your librarian friend and an article in Discover."

"Oh that pesky article again."

"Edward I owe you an apology. I ran away from you last Saturday when I really didn't want to. I'm sorry. I thought I'd never see you again."

"There's little chance of that. I worried that you would never want to see me again. I thought you would slap me when I kissed you. I'd never done anything that bold in my whole life. I just couldn't help myself. When you said the name Isaac I guessed you had read the Discover article. Almost a year ago, I buried Isaac and replaced him with Edward. I underwent painful plastic surgery to do that. Isaac became a very unhappy man. He felt pressured to invent weapons for the military to keep his hyperspace project going. When Isaac invented weapons, the death of all the people who would die from them weighed on his mind as the nuclear bomb weighed on Oppenheimer and his scientists. All Isaac ever wanted to do is to play music and share it with someone special. Edward is determined to do just that and thanks to you he did last week."

"I like Edward better than Isaac, but I'm worried that this private eye/detective will find you. If an amateur like me could figure out who you are, he surely will."

"Mary Ann, I just want to spend time with you. I don't care about anything else. I will avoid the government as best I can but if they find me I'll refuse to help them. They can't make me do something I don't want to do."

"They seem to want to try. How did you get in this mess?"

"All I cared about is the hyperspace project. I have always believed that the exploration and colonization of space is essential to the survival of our species. We just face too many cosmic and earth bound disasters like comets, asteroids, massive solar ejections, Nova's and super volcanoes to depend on this one planet. For the first several years, everyone seemed to be happy with the hyperspace projector I developed and how it allowed us to colonize the solar system. Then a series of unfortunate incidents changed everything.

"First, the Discover article appeared. A low-level lab technician provided the information to Discover and convinced them to run it. The technician lost his job but the damage had been done. Everyone wanted to know about the project but our government continued to deny its existence except of course to Members of Congress. They had to be briefed which led to more leaks. It became the best-known secret in the world.

"Then out of the blue a Special Forces team attacked our facility and attempted to take it over. We thwarted the attack because of our tight security and the intervention of a larger army force from a nearby base but the Special Forces team came close to taking the facility. We believe the Chinese were behind the attack but the few remaining members of the attack force, who were of mixed races refused to reveal who sent them even after enhanced interrogation techniques.

"After that, the military took over our project. They shut the hyperspace projector down, stranding thousands of colonists and scientists, on Mars, Ganymede, Titan, Europa, and our moon. The largest colony, Mars had some ability to be self sustaining but the rest of the colonies had no such ability. The colonists on Europa could only survive for two weeks after the shut down. I quickly finished my design of an advanced laser system and an energy shield to protect the facility and allay the military's concerns. I had been working on these systems for several years but had never finished them. I worried that the military would use them to dominate and kill people in other parts of the world. When the systems worked in tests at the facility, the military allowed the hyperspace projector to re-open. The scientists and the colonists once again started receiving the food, water, fuel and oxygen they needed to survive.

"The military of course wanted these technologies and undoubtedly closed the hyperspace facility to force me to develop them. They put an enormous amount of pressure on me including physical threats to adapt the lasers to their weapons systems and to develop military energy shields. They had lasers but they were primitive by comparison. I adapted the lasers for their attack jets and naval ships but refused to further develop the energy shields, which could completely change the balance of power in the world. I soon realized I couldn't continue to design these terrible weapons. I left the facility, obtained plastic surgery and disappeared into the homeless world. Like the hyperspace projector the lasers and energy shields need periodic adjustments to work properly. I did some work on a self-adjusting program for each of the systems but never completed the programing for any of the systems.

"After I became homeless I continued to provide the adjustments to the projector to keep it working but have not done so for the lasers on the jets, ships and at the facility or for the facility energy shield. As a result they may no longer work or if they do not very well. The military has tried to use other scientists to provide the adjustments and to adapt my work but so far no one has been able to do so. All three systems are based on my three dimensional math system, which is almost impossible to understand without proper instruction and training. Before I left, I didn't have the opportunity to train anyone, nor is it likely I would have trained anyone if I had the time. Still, I developed three friends and fellow scientists and mathematicians at the Fermilab facility: Ted, Tom and Peter. They shared my devotion to the hyperspace project, but I never trusted them completely. When I left the facility I worked with them on problems associated with the hyperspace projector and with adjusting the projector when needed. Then when they asked for a meeting three months after I left, I wisely stayed at a distance and studied the meeting site before I revealed myself. The site crawled with FBI and local police. They intended to betray me. From this moment forward, I knew the military, the FBI and local police would pursue me and use whatever means they could to trap me. I expect other nations would do the same thing. I'm the only one with the answers they seek. I learned not to trust anyone."

"Edward this sounds like science fiction. How are you able to do this?"

"I don't really know. I just look at a problem and start developing solutions. If I run into a roadblock I just invent ways to get around the problems. The funny thing is that the systems I develop almost always work. From an engineering point of view, this is almost impossible. I should fail a hundred times before I succeed."

"And you, the most important scientist in the world, wants to make music and spend time with me?"

"Yes that is all I want to do. Anything else I do will create more problems than it solves. I want my inventions to help people throughout the world, not give some people power over others. Also, I want to have a normal relationship with a woman. I'm not a computer. I'm a human being."

"That actually makes some sense. Let's put all that science fiction stuff aside. So what do we do now that we are downtown on a Saturday morning?"

"We walk, talk and make music for all of those who will listen. I have a guitar stashed away at DePaul we can use. The world will be our special place. We just have to use it."

"Lead on entertainer. I just want to have fun for a few hours and not plan anything. I had a long week at work."

"Ha I had a long week as a homeless person. You'd be surprised what I did."

"Nothing you did will surprise me."

Mary Ann and Edward had another magical day. They walked along the lake. Edward played guitar as they strolled, Mary Ann providing accompaniment. Edward borrowed a street musician's violin on Michigan Avenue and played a Mozart concerto. They both danced and sang to some street drummers. They sat in the park next to the Art Institute and listened to the birds and people. Mary Ann and Edward ate food from street vendors, pretending to be at the Taste of Chicago.

They even spent time at Buckingham fountain in Grant Park, letting droplets of water cool them. Time just seemed to float pass. When Edward finally accompanied Mary Ann to her condo, she surprised herself by saying.

"Edward I don't want this day to end. Do you want to come upstairs with me?"

"Of course I do. Whenever I can spend time with you I will. I told you I loved you and I meant it."

"Edward, remember what you just said. I may hold you to it."

"I hope you do." Edward replied.

When Edward and Mary Ann passed Randolph on the way up the elevator, he only smiled. Within minutes, Mary Ann and Edward kissed inside her apartment. Mary Ann broke away for a moment.

"Edward I don't understand it. I have romantic feelings for you even though you're not like the boys I usually date."

"Mary Ann you're overthinking everything. Life doesn't always give us opportunities to be close to someone else. This is our time. Even though I want to be intimate with you, I'll be almost as happy in your arms all night. I just want to be close to the woman I love."

"And I to you. And you don't have to worry about the intimacy part. I want to have sex with you. Even though I have no plans to become pregnant, a girl could do a lot worse than having a baby with the smartest man on earth."

"Ha I should have used that line before, but there hasn't been a before. You're the first woman I've loved."

As Mary Ann came into Edward's arms she said.

"If you had used that line it would have been the first original one I have heard in years."

In the morning, a happy Mary Ann woke to find Edward absent from her bed. She smelled coffee in her small kitchen. She quickly took care of her bathroom needs, slipped on a robe and joined Edward at the kitchen table. Edward used her laptop as a maestro might conduct an orchestra.

"Mary Ann I hope you don't mind. I found your password and am working on a present for you. Okay I think I'm done. You are now the proud owner of the penthouse upstairs, well at least a dummy corporation owned by you is. A beautiful woman like you should have a little more space."

"The penthouse is beautiful but expensive. It has been on the market for a while. Why would you buy it for me? Can you afford it?"

"Thanks to my one hundred patents, I'm very wealthy. Money pours into my accounts every month. And as a homeless person my expenses aren't exactly high. Buying that condo for you barely made a dent in my finances. Anyway, we need to have a second place to help avoid the detectives and private eyes. I will come and go. We should use both places for now. Who knows what the future will bring?"

"Can I decorate it?"

"Of course, I'll give you an allowance. I want you to be comfortable. Now what do you want to do today?"

"I don't know. Let's have a day like yesterday. There is a whole world to explore."

"You read my mind."

THE PURSUERS

Rich Richardson with his secretary assistant Rose Thompson escorted the two FBI men into Rich Richardson's small private detective office. The men looked very intense and not prone to making small talk. They showed their FBI credentials as they walked inside. The larger one spoke immediately upon taking a chair facing Rich Richardson's small cluttered desk.

"We're looking for an important scientist, critical to our national defense. He disappeared about a year ago from our research facility at the old Fermilab site in Batavia. Our internal efforts to find him have met with little success. We believe he is still in the Chicago area. We are told you are the man to see if we are looking for someone, particularly in this area. We will pay you $200 per hour plus expenses. We will also pay you up to $100,000 as a bonus for finding this scientist in the next month. The sooner you find him the higher the bonus. Are you interested?"

"Yes of course I am. If he is not in this area any longer, do I have your permission to search for him elsewhere?"

"Yes ", the smaller man said. "Do whatever you have to do but find this man."

"You've come to the right man and of course woman assistant. Finding people is what I do. I will, of course, need to have everything you have on the missing scientist. I would also like to interview the people at his place of work. I assume I will need some kind of access to do so. When I have this information, I can begin. Oh and I would like a $5000 retainer to begin work."

"I have a check here for $10,000 and a retention contract. If you sign it, I will give you the check and we can begin. The Director of the FBI is involved in this matter. Finding this scientist is a very high priority. I'll call the old Fermilab laboratory and make an appointment for you. Oh and we want bi weekly updates on your progress." The larger man said.

"Sounds fair. I assume you left your contact information in the materials in your hand." Steve said.

"Yes our cards are in here. I think this concludes our business. Just sign the retention agreement and we can begin."

"I wonder should I have my attorney look at this?"

"No. We're the FBI. We don't do amendments to our contracts. Sign the agreement or we will get someone else to do the work." The smaller man said.

"Oh if you say it that way, of course I will sign."

When the men left, Rich Richardson stared at his beautiful assistant for several minutes then said.

"Wow that national security stuff is pretty creepy but how could I turn down a rich contract like this one. I don't think those FBI guys are telling us everything. If this scientist is as important as they say I doubt we will be the only one looking for him. I sense some danger here. I have a nose for it after all those years on the force. Rose I don't want to expose you too much to this kind of thing."

"Rich this goes along with the job. Didn't that guy who was cheating on his wife pull a shotgun. Danger is what we do. Now let's get organized so we can get a good start on this job."

"We will as soon as I take out a beautiful woman for a nice lunch. I suddenly feel flush with cash."

"That's okay with me. I could do with a little attention." Rose laughed.

As Rose and Rich left for a nice lunch, Susan Wang, a very beautiful woman of Chinese ancestry, watched them very carefully from a car across the street. Susan's world recently imploded but she bore little responsibility for the tragedy. Until the age of twenty-four, her life had been one of accomplishment and great happiness. With a Brown degree in Math and Economics and a MBA from Harvard, Susan received a wonderful offer from a prestigious hedge fund on Wall Street. She also had a nice marriage proposal from a Jason Brown a Wall Street lawyer. She loved Jason and everything about her life. Then out of the blue her father sat down with her one day. She remembered the conversation as if it still took place.

"Susan when we came to this country the Chinese government approached us. They said we had always been loyal to the government and communist way of life and could continue to be of service. As a longtime importer and exporter, they assumed we would set up the same business in America. If we did so, they would make sure our company received favorable export and import treatment from the Chinese government. We would be assured of great success. In return, they wanted me to keep my eyes and ears open for anything that I came to know that would be of value to the Chinese government. I passed along a few pieces of information over the years and as you know became a very successful businessman.

"Last week a member of the Chinese Consulate in Chicago visited me. He said that they had begun a new program of turning American born Chinese into spies for the Chinese government. The consulate official said you Susan had been selected for the program. They asked me to persuade you to join. If I complied and you joined, I would continue to prosper. If you did not, they would leak information to the US government of my spy activities. They would also withdraw favorable treatment of the goods I imported or exported and instead impose bureaucratic impediments on everything I imported or exported. I would be bankrupt in a matter of months. This Chinese official then bowed and left. You must do this for us, our family. You have to spy for the Chinese. Otherwise we face ruin and I face prison time."

Although she protested and at first refused, Susan eventually agreed to join the Chinese clandestine service. She really had no choice. Her life had become a nightmare ever since. Susan lost her boyfriend trying to work at the hedge fund, spying for the Chinese and using what little time she had left to work on her relationship. After losing the love of her life, she also had to quit her hedge fund job. The Chinese government just became too demanding of her time. Susan of course had plenty of money. Her father's firm made more money than ever and at the insistence of her Chinese handlers much of it went to her, but Susan felt terrible about betraying the country she had come to love.

Susan followed the FBI agents to Rich Richardson's agency. Her Chinese contacts informed her these agents worked on the missing American scientist case. A quick search of the Internet informed Susan that Rich had a reputation as one of the best detectives in Chicago. Susan would follow Rich and let this skilled person lead her to the American scientist. Her handlers had pushed her very hard on this assignment. Susan had to inform the Chinese kidnap team of the whereabouts of this scientist, so they could drug the scientist and take him to China.

Rich laughed as he left his office. Rich hoped the beautiful Chinese spy enjoyed watching he and Rose go to lunch. A man possessed of an extraordinary eye for detail, Steve spotted the woman almost immediately. Beautiful Chinese women did not as a rule watch his shabby offices in a marginal area of the city. Her government, assuming she spied for China, would want this scientist as much as the U.S. Rich wondered what other foreign governments would be out there looking. For the first time since the FBI men came, Rich began to have some apprehensions about his new job. Foreign government spies didn't always respect the laws of the countries where they operated. They would kill to get what they wanted with little fear of the consequences.

THE PLAN

Edward and Mary Ann sat on their long penthouse balcony overlooking Lake Michigan and began a serious conversation. "Edward I haven't been back to the homeless pantry. If I go there, the detective will question me and follow me back to this building. Frankly, I'm surprised he hasn't found this place already." Mary Ann sighed.

"We've been lucky so far. The girls at your pantry haven't given us up, but if the FBI shows up I wonder whether they will continue to protect you. Citing national security they might be able to get a search warrant for your pantry's employment records. They will find you," Edward said.

"Yes, I know. The question is what happens then? We have it arranged with the people who work the front desk to call me on my cell if anyone wants to see me. If they do I can go down the elevator to my apartment while you stay here. It should work."

"Yeah it'll work but what then? Will the detective or someone else stake out the building? Sooner or later they will see me entering. If I stay at my satellite apartment, they can follow you to me. I think we have some time but how much I don't know."

"I'm still not clear what happens when they find you. You are not a felon. They have no right to take you."

"When national security is involved, no one has any rights. They will make up charges if they don't have any. If I won't cooperate, they will threaten you. They will do anything to control me."

"We could move to another country."

"I thought of that. In those countries I would have even fewer rights. They would do the same thing. I should never have designed weapons. I feel very stupid for having done so."

"You did what you had to do to save your very important project. My god because of your genius, we have men living on Mars and some of the largest moons in the solar system. It's amazing what you have done."

"The military doesn't care. All they care about is being the biggest and strongest military force in the world. They seek power as do the politicians who control them."

"What can we do?"

"As long as the laser and shield systems need periodic adjustment, I have leverage on the military and the government. They need me. I've thought about installing self-adjustment software in the computers that control these systems but if I do, they won't need me so much. They may decide to consolidate their gains by eliminating me. In that way, no one else can have the weapons. I could give the technology to the world but that would start an arms race with possibly dire consequences. I can, however, threaten to give the systems to the world if they harm us in any way. Our government may, however, decide to call my bluff knowing that for the reasons above, I probably wouldn't publish the technology. So for now, I will continue to hide and withhold the weapon adjustment protocols. I don't know what else to do."

"What do you want to do about us?"

"Marry you, be with you, love you, and give you everything I have."

"Is that a proposal?"

"Yes."

"I don't know. Being with you is risky even foolish, but for reasons I don't really understand it seems right for me. I had the opportunity to marry the perfect man, handsome, smart, successful and sure to give me a comfortable life full of babies and country clubs. Yet, I felt like I would drown in that world, so I rejected it. You on the other hand, offer me a life full of risk, possible fame, music performances and excitement.

"Frankly, I'm a little scared. Sinister and soulless soldiers hunting us won't allow me a restful night sleep. Still, the great men of history or women for that matter require a spouse to support and stabilize them. They become an essential part of their greatness. I once wrote a paper on it in college. Almost none of the great figures would have made it without this support. If I play this role, I can make a difference. I sure won't make any difference sipping cocktails at country clubs. All my life people have spoken of my beauty, which I really didn't have anything to do with creating. They never recognize or seem to care that I work hard and am talented and smart. With you I can be what I make of myself. Heck, if we decide to have children, I could do worse than having the smartest man on earth as their father. So, I guess what I am saying is yes." Mary Ann said with a smile on her face.

"I understand you. If you substitute the word smart for beautiful we have similar experiences. And you are absolutely correct about my needing a supportive spouse. Without you I don't think I can make it. So if it is okay with you, we will go to Las Vegas and marry as soon as we can pack. For security reasons we can't tell anyone, but there is no reason for us to delay."

"What about my job?"

"We don't need the money but for security reasons you may want to ask for a leave of absence to attend the funeral of a loved one. If detectives and agents are hot on our tail, this may give you some cover."

"I'll ask tomorrow but where will we go after the wedding?"

"I have homes near Glacier National Park in Montana and Eielson Air Force Base in Alaska. We'll spend some time at these large homes with large acreage. They're remote, and the people there will not be as nosy as they might be in other places. With my sophisticated electronic equipment we will be able to make music and broadcast it to a large audience without being traced. If things die down a little, we might be able to perform locally."

"Sounds great. I'll quit my job after the wedding then. This is a big risk for me, but all I really ever waned to do was to perform. Now I can." Mary Ann laughed.

"Mary Ann, the government is forcing us to do this. If I had a choice I would stay here with you and do the same thing we are doing now."

"So would I except I might want to perform a little more than we have."

CHICAGO HUNT

After a nice lunch at Gibson's Steakhouse, Rich began to bounce his thoughts off of Rose as he always did.

"Rose if I am a scientist and need to disappear how do I do it, particularly if I want to stay in the Chicago Area."

"With thousands of cameras everywhere you go and new advanced facial recognition software, I don't know how you can. Even if you're careful, a camera you don't see will pick up your image. I'm sure the FBI has accessed many of these cameras and thousands of hours of footage, but they wouldn't have approached us if they found anything." Rose answered.

"Exactly. So there is only one possible answer. Isaac must have altered his appearance."

"He would, of course, wear disguises. But that might not be enough. No a better approach for him would be to have plastic surgery, enough so that the facial recognition programs wouldn't identify him. Also, he would look more natural and less suspicious. Disguises can look pretty phony if you don't do them right. Even if he had the surgery, he wouldn't be able to change his age, his body type, and the way he walks. To a person looking for him, they might still be able to recognize him when a computer wouldn't."

"Right again. He would have to stay off the grid so to speak. Isaac would have to be involved in something where people wouldn't pay attention to him. What might that be?"

"I haven't a clue. Maybe he would work in some menial job and live simply, something like that." Rose said.

"No I don't think so. Jobs require a great deal of paperwork, which he would have to fake. They also reduce your flexibility. He has no need of money. At the same time, he would stand out if he simply did nothing. Unless of course, he is part of a group that does nothing."

"What does that mean?"

"The homeless, yes of course, the homeless population would provide perfect cover for him. No one even sees them. He would be invisible." Rich said with a big smile on his face.

"Yes, plastic surgery plus living in the homeless community would explain how he has avoided detection for so long. He may not be there but it is a good place to start."

"And so we will. We could go to the homeless areas in the city, their neighborhoods or to the free food pantries. Let's start with the pantries. Everyone has to eat. Can you find me a list?"

"Of course, I will prepare one as soon as we return. Now let's enjoy the rest of our delicious lunch." Rose said with a laugh.

Over the next two weeks, Rich visited several pantries and even stopped by some homeless areas. At the third pantry, Rich encountered a particularly talkative man named Butch.

"Rich is that your name. I'm Butch. It's nice to meet a real private detective and a former Chicago Police Detective. When I can find a TV I like to watch detective stories."

"Yeah you can help me on an important case and act like a real detective. The FBI is involved. An important scientist went missing. We think he might have ended up in the homeless community. This is his picture. He may have changed his appearance to avoid being recognized." Rich said.

"Wow what did he do wrong?"

"Nothing really. We just want to find him."

"Yeah we have a lot of smart but crazy people in the community. Let me think. I'm having one of my rare clear moments. I actually practiced law for a while, well sort of. I was a bail bondsman. There is one guy I heard about. He makes elaborate cardboard houses to sleep in. He is supposedly young like this guy, but I never met him. They call him the architect. He shows up at some of the pantries one in particular but seldom stays in the same place."

"Sounds like him. Where is this pantry?"

"On the West side, I'll give you the address, but I'm going to have to get it from the nice lady over there. I don't remember numbers very well anymore. I've been there several times. They make a great beef stew." Butch said.

"Thanks I appreciate that, so much so that I'm gong to give you a ten dollar bill." Rich said.

"Great, I know just what I can buy with it."

A day later, after interviewing the tough middle age woman at the pantry, Rich returned to his car, which faced the front end of the pantry. As he ate his sandwich, he carefully watched everyone coming into the facility.

At 2 PM when the last homeless men and women began leaving the facility, Rich re-entered the pantry.

He found Roberta organizing the clean up and immediately confronted her.

"I watched everyone coming and going. Some homeless people told me a young well kept man they call the architect eats here, but I didn't see him."

"I didn't either but that's the way it is here. While we have regulars, they don't come every week. Sometimes regulars will simply disappear. We ask about them but don't always receive straight answers. This so-called architect guy if you and I are thinking of the same person just didn't come today. Maybe he will come next week." Roberta said.

"Where is the beautiful young woman who worked here? I didn't see her leave."

"She came early and left early. She likes to work that way and as a volunteer we don't object. We need the help." Roberta said.

"But how did she get passed me?"

"She uses the back door. It is closer to where she keeps her car. She has an arrangement with a local body shop two blocks away to park her car." Roberta answered.

"It seems too convenient to me. I show up and suddenly two people who should be here aren't." Rich said in a very irritated tone.

"Look, this is a homeless pantry. We are all volunteers on the weekend. We don't tend to date or otherwise spend time with the poor unfortunate people who come here. We just provide them meals and then go about our normal lives. Come another time and you'll probably find the people you want. As to some kind of conspiracy to keep these people from you, that is ridiculous. I'm a litigation attorney and here enough of this stuff in my regular job."

"I assure you I will return."

"You're welcome as is everyone else as long as you don't disrupt our operation." Roberta said walking away from Rich.

Rich left the pantry in a foul mood. Although he had no proof whatsoever, his detective nose told him that the beautiful young woman intercepted the architect and took him someplace else to protect him. Why she would do this he did not know but he would find out."

LAS VEGAS

Edward and Mary Ann married in Los Vegas hours after they landed there. They couldn't wait. The marriage mill they used, Happy Beginnings produced legal and efficient weddings. Also, they didn't ask a lot of questions. After the ceremony, where the so-called pastor kept talking about Mary Ann's great beauty, the so-called ultimate babe and how they could use her to make money, the impatient couple returned to a beautiful room at the Venetian. Mary Ann couldn't take one more minute of the so-called pastor. They immediately ordered Champagne and an expensive meal and relaxed in each other's arms. Edward and Mary Ann didn't want to go anywhere. They made love and talked about the wonderful future they would have together making and recording music.

THE DISAPPEARING LEAD

Meanwhile in Chicago, the short FBI man named Ted who Rich decided must have an Napolean complex accompanied Rich to the West Side food pantry. With a little research, Rich discovered that the director of the pantry would be in her office but the bossy and smart woman lawyer wouldn't be. By using his badge, Rich hoped that Ted would find out the address of the beautiful woman volunteer. She knew where the scientist hid. He would bet his next check from the FBI on it.

Sue, the Director of the Food Pantry's office after looking at Ted's FBI badge showed Rich and Ted into her office. Seconds after entering the director's office, Rich asked a question.

"You have a beautiful woman volunteer working here on Saturdays. Her name is Mary Ann. Do you have any information on her full name and address? She hasn't done anything wrong but we need to talk to her and don't know where to find her."

"Oh Yes, Mary Ann Winston. Her address should be on this computer. Yes, here it is. 453 N. Lake Shore Drive, Apartment 520. Mary Ann lists her regular job as working for a public relations company in the city but she left no further information. When you look like Mary Ann you have to be careful what kind of information you leave. Even so she seems like a nice woman volunteer, but I haven't seen her after I approved her as a volunteer. Why on earth do you want to talk to her?"

"FBI business, it has nothing to do with you. Thank you for your help. By the way, did you see Mary Ann with one of your homeless clients? Here is his picture but he may have changed his appearance." Ted said.

"No I don't know this man nor have I heard anything about him being with Mary Ann. It is highly unlikely that a great beauty like Mary Ann would have been dating a homeless man. I can ask some of the volunteer staff what they know. Who should I call?" Sue said.

"Me. We would appreciate that very much." Rich said.

"Okay always happy to help the FBI. My great uncle Frank worked for the FBI before your time." Sue said casually

"That's great Sue. The bureau depends on people like you for our investigations." Ted said.

After they left, Rich turned to Ted.

"She doesn't seem to know very much. Hopefully she will talk to her staff and find out more. Do you want to come to Mary Ann's address with me?"

"No that is your job. I will join you only when needed such as now. Let me know what happens at Mary Ann's high rise."

"I will Ted," Rich said as he walked toward his car. Rich immediately called Rose with the public relations reference and asked her to see what she could find. Rose poured through the major firms in the city listed in Crain's Chicago Business seeing if she could find Mary Ann. Most firms now included pictures and resumes of their employees to attract customers. So when she found a likely firm she Googled it. Two hours later as Rich sipped a cup of coffee, Rose found Mary Ann's work address after hours of intensive research. Rich as usual marveled at his resourceful assistant. Tomorrow he would interview the people in Mary Ann's firm. He would then find out where this woman hid. But first he had to visit May Ann's apartment building. Rich might get lucky and find Mary Ann there but somehow he doubted it.

Rich approached the large muscular black man behind the counter to the entrance of the high rise. Rich noticed the man's callous covered knuckles, as those belonging to a boxer. A dispute with this man would not end well for you unless you could bring a weapon to bear on him.

"Hi my name is Rich. I'm a former Chicago police detective and a licensed private detective. The FBI has hired me to find a missing scientist named Isaac. A resident of your building, Mary Ann Winston, has been seen in the company of a man who might be this scientist. I would like to question her to see what she knows."

"I'm sorry Miss Winston is not in at the moment. I can leave a message for her if you have a card." The big black man said cautiously.

"Could you call up to her apartment please? I know that these high rises have back doors that the residents sometimes use." Rich said.

"I could do that but this is a work day for her. She left this morning at the usual time. I ordinarily don't see her until 7 pm. Her job keeps her late."

"Still, I would like you to ring her. My information is that she lives in apartment 520."

"Okay." The large black man said as he rung Mary Ann's apartment. After many rings, the man put this phone back in its cradle.

"As I said she is not here and the system does not allow me to leave a message."

"Okay here is my card. Will you make sure Mary Ann receives it?"

"Sure. We leave the cards in the tenant's mailboxes when the mail is loaded into them. Is there anything else I can do?"

"Yes, this is a picture of the missing scientist. Have you seen him around here?"

The big black man stared at the picture and slowly shook his head. "No can't say that I have."

"Surely Mary Ann has men coming through here. Beautiful women always do."

"Yes but not this guy. My job is not to pry into a tenant's private life."

"I wonder if I could look at your video recordings to see if I recognize this guy. Also, I would like to look at Mary Ann's apartment if at all possible." Rich said pleasantly.

"No and no. You will need a warrant to look at the tape or to go through Mary Ann's apartment. I am not authorized to allow you to do either one." The black man said his anger building.

"Well then I will have to obtain a warrant won't I?" Rich said.

"Yes you will."

"Okay I will return near the time Mary Ann comes home from work. I will catch her then." Rich said happily as he left the front desk area, but as he did so, Rich left a small microphone in a plant near the desk. Rich stepped outside and listened to the microphone on his cell phone. He didn't have to wait long.

"A private detective named Rich came to see you. He says he works with the FBI. He is going to wait for you to come home from work. I thought you ought to know." After a few seconds, the big man continued. "Okay, will do."

Rich shook his head. The big man showed some sophistication. He said very little. Perhaps the man noticed Rich, putting the microphone in the planter. The big man presumably talked to Mary Ann. Rich thought about going back into the high rise and confronting the big man but decided not to do so right away. He would as he promised return, but he would probably not see Mary Ann. If she had something to hide she would not return at her regular time. Rich needed to talk to Ted to see if he could obtain a warrant. If not, he had to use what he had or what he might record in the next few hours to leverage more information from the big man. This man obviously knew a great deal more about Mary Ann and the scientist than he shared with Rich.

When Rich returned to the high rise at about 6pm, he parked in a space, which allowed him to observe the front door. For an hour and a half he watched as a large number of residents entered. None of them remotely matched his description of Isaac nor did any of them resemble Mary Ann. His microphone no longer worked. Apparently, the big man found and destroyed it. Also, Rich once again became aware of the beautiful Asian woman. She watched the same door as he did. In fact, she preceded him in observing the front door. The Asian woman already sat there watching when he arrived. At eight, Rich finally decided to stop observing the front door. Frustrated, he once again approached the big man behind the desk. He casually said.

"Do you remember me?"

"Yeah you're the guy who left the illegal bug. I called our attorney about that after I destroyed it. Did you find out anything interesting?"

"You called Mary Ann after I left. So you knew all along where she was. I expect you warned her not to come back to her apartment."

"I said nothing of the kind. As you know, I merely mentioned that you had come looking for her."

"Where is she? You must know."

"As a matter of fact, I don't know. She didn't tell me. It's none of my business."

"Do you know where Mary works or the names of any of her friends or colleagues?"

"I don't know her friends. As to her place of employment, it's in our records but without a warrant I can't give it to you. If you knew to come here why don't you know where she works?"

"Even though the homeless pantry form she filled out asked for the information she didn't provide it. I don't know why. The homeless pantry was so desperate for volunteers they overlooked it. Is she friendly with anyone in the building? They may know more."

"Not that I know. Most of the people who live here keep to themselves." The big man responded.

"I know you are stonewalling me. I'll bring an FBI agent next time I come. Maybe you will be more helpful next time." Rich said as he stormed out of the door.

Rich needed to be patient. Perhaps Mary Ann's place of work would help.

The large public relations firm had nice offices in a facility just north of downtown in the river east area of Chicago. The intensity of the place became immediately apparent. Young and middle aged people ran around ducking in and out of meetings, answering phones and text messages and looking and acting very stressed. Rich could easily imagine the Mary Ann he briefly met occupying this space. He found a man who appeared to be in charge and casually approached him before the man could plow into another meeting.

"Hi I'm Rich. I'm a former CPD Detective and licensed private investigator working for the FBI. I'm trying to locate Mary Ann Winston. Here is a letter the Assistant Director of the FBI gave me. Mary Ann befriended an important government scientist who we would like to locate. I'm told she works here."

The middle-aged man eyed Rich closely then shrugged.

"Mary Ann is on vacation. I've been telling her for years to use up her vacation time. She finally took me up on my offer. Mary Ann kind of surprised me when she did. My name is Abbott by the way."

"Abbott do you know where she went?"

"No she didn't tell me. She seemed a little nervous and excited." Abbott said.

"Does she have any friends in the office she might have told?" Rich asked.

"Mary Ann is very focused. Guys hit on her all the time but she brushes them off. As to girls, she sometimes talks to Terry, a girl that handles accounts like she does. With everyone else, it's business and casual conversation. Come on, Terry is over here." Abbott said.

Abbott showed them to Terry's station. A cute small petite redhead, Terry spoke with a man on the screen. Abbott interrupted.

"Terry can you take a minute. This man is working with the FBI. He wants to talk to you about Mary Ann."

Speaking to the man on the screen, Terry said. "Hey Salam, I've got to go. Remember I need the data on the mouthwash trial before I can finish up the ad proofs."

With Salam suddenly disappearing from the screen. Terry turned toward Rich.

"Mary Ann is on vacation. You'll have to wait until she returns to talk with her."

"Do you know where she went?"

"No she wouldn't tell me. Usually Mary Ann tells me things but this time she wouldn't despite my best efforts to persuade her. She usually isn't like that. It must be a guy, but I have no idea who. She attracts so many men. I don't know where to send you. She had a serious boyfriend when she first started here but they broke up two years ago. She hasn't talked about him since then." Terry said.

"How about other girlfriends like you. Do you know of any?" Rich asked.

"Yeah Tiffany. Mary Ann might have said something to her. They've been friends since college. I met her once. She is a cute blond that sells industrial equipment. I don't know where. By the way, why do you want to find her so badly? Mary Ann is a very nice hard working person. Looking the way she does, Mary Ann could be stuck up and difficult. She is neither."

"We think she is with an important government scientist, who we would very much like to find. We find her we find him." Rich said.

"Doesn't sound like Mary Ann. When she dates, which isn't often, she dates the hottest guys out there. This scientist doesn't sound like that kind of guy." Terry said.

"He isn't but they have apparently spent some time together. It's the only solid lead I have." Rich said.

"Oh wait a minute. I have an idea. Mary Ann goes pretty religiously to the East Bank Club. She likes to keep fit. You might find out more about her there. She mentioned going out on a date with a guy from there but when I asked about the guy after they went out, she said their relationship ended before it began. Mary Ann is very picky about the guys she dates." Terry said.

"Does Tiffany go to the club?"

"I think so. They have good deals for young people just starting on their careers. I think Tiffany and Mary Ann are both on one of those deals. I joined for a while but it got too expensive for me. May Ann worried about the cost too."

"Yeah okay. I'll ask around for Tiffany and this guy she dated at the club. I've been a member there off and on. It's a little expensive for me too, but you can make good contacts. I've been thinking about starting my membership again." Rich said.

An hour later Rich with a day's pass in hand, walked around the East Bank Club. He spoke with some of the staff he remembered from his work out days. The staff all recognized Mary Ann, the incredible babe, when he showed them a picture, but they didn't know her very well. They also recognized Tiffany as a member but like Mary Ann they didn't know much about her. Neither girl worked out in the huge facility that day. Then Rich received a break. One of the instructors mentioned a guy who dated Mary Ann. He gave him 45 minutes of instruction 5 times a week. He had a session with the guy in 35 minutes. This guy, Tim, could probably be found on one of the step or walking machines warming up his muscles.

Rich had no problem locating Tim. A modern version of Cary Grant, the guy looked like a movie star. He also had a great physique from his frequent and hard workouts. Rich approached him casually.

"Tim, my name is Rich, I'm a former Chicago Detective turned private eye. The FBI hired me to find an important scientist named Isaac. This is his picture. He may have undergone plastic surgery. Apparently, Mary Ann Winston knows a guy that fits this person's description. We wanted to talk with her. Since you dated her, I thought you might have her number or know something about her friend Tiffany."

Tim stopped peddling for a while then responded to Rich's question. "Mary Ann is the most beautiful woman I have ever seen. She is also smart, nice, fun and apparently a good singer. She isn't even a 10 on a 10 point scale; she is an 11. I dated her one time. I drank too much at our dinner and became a little aggressive when I took her home. As a result, our date ended badly. She has refused to talk with me ever since. She even changed her cell number."

"Do you happen to know her friend Tiffany?"

"Yes as a matter of fact I do. Tiffany is very cute, not in Mary Ann's league but definitely worth some male attention. When I dated Mary Ann, she double dated with us. I managed to get her card and programed her number into my phone in case things didn't work out with Mary Ann. I called her after my disastrous date with Mary Ann but she wouldn't take my call. I got the hint. I knew she liked me but apparently Mary Ann blackballed me with her. I have her number right here. As far as I know, this number is still good. Her last name is Robbins." Tim said.

"Thanks, Tim I appreciate the information." Rich said.

"Hey if you talk to Tiffany can you tell her I'm not such a bad guy after all." Tim said.

"Sure Tim. I will. Thanks for the info."

Rich reached Tiffany the 6th time he called her. Tiffany sounded a little contrite when she spoke.

"Rich I'm sorry I didn't call you back. I know you work for the FBI and all. How can I help you? You said you were looking for a lost scientist. Mary Ann isn't exactly the science type."

"We believe she met the scientist at the West Side Food Pantry. Mary Ann volunteered there. We have been trying to locate Mary Ann but have so far been unsuccessful. We heard that she just took some vacation time but the people at her work didn't know where she went."

"I don't know either. She isn't even answering her phone. I've called her several times. All I know is that she seemed very excited when she left. Mary Ann doesn't take a lot of vacations and this one came up very quickly." Tiffany said.

"Tiffany do you have her phone number? I'll give her a call. She might answer me."

"I don't know if I should. You are just a voice on the phone. You could be anyone. Mary Ann has trouble with guys calling and harassing her. She recently changed her phone number to avoid them. If I gave out her number I would be defeating what she has tried to do." Tiffany said.

"Okay we can meet somewhere and I can show you my credentials. In that way, you'll believe me. What place is convenient for you?" Rich said.

"The East Bank Club tomorrow at 5. I'll be working out there then." Tiffany said.

The next day, Tiffany met Rich in her workout outfit. She wanted to look good for this private eye if indeed he happened to be one.

"Hi I'm Rich. Here is my private eye identification, a letter from the assistant director of the FBI and my former CPD police ID. If necessary,

I have an FBI agent ready to answer a phone call to verify that they have hired me."

"You certainly get to the point. Your ID's looks legitimate. I looked them up online before I came here so I can recognize a fake ID. You can't be too careful. Okay her cell number is 3125654003. I don't know if she will answer you. She doesn't answer calls from strangers she doesn't recognize. Neither do I."

"Could you call her and verify who I am?" Rich asked.

"Sure. I can do that, but she isn't answering my phone calls. So all I can do is leave a message. I'll do it before I leave here today." Tiffany replied.

"Is this usual, her not answering your calls?"

"No, but if she is with a guy I can see it. She is a private person and will only talk when she is ready." Tiffany said.

"Will you contact me if she calls? Here is my card." Rich said.

"Yeah sure, I can do that." Tiffany said taking Rich's card.

After the last statement, Rich looked a little uncomfortable. He looked as if he wanted to ask another question but instead said.

"Thanks for your help Tiffany. Getting in touch with Mary Ann is a matter of national security. We have to find that scientist. I'll be back in touch." Shaking Tiffany's hand, Rich turned and rapidly left. Tiffany stared after him with a puzzled look on her face. Tiffany liked the detective's looks but his intensity made her a little uncomfortable.

THE END OF THE HONEYMOON.

The call from Tiffany followed by a call from Rich, both of which went to Mary Ann's voice mail, abruptly ended Edward and Mary Ann's honeymoon. With Edward's help, Mary Ann immediately changed her cell phone number and her cell carrier. For Edward, this had been the happiest time of his life. While Mary Ann and Edward only gambled a little, Edward with his brilliant mind had a way of winning that attracted too much attention. As a result, Edward and Tiffany found other ways to entertain themselves. They walked miles down the various Vegas streets, swam in the pool, read novels and attended show after show at the various casinos. They also enjoyed some of the best meals they had ever eaten. With Edward's wealth and his uncanny ability to win at the casinos, neither of them worried about the money they spent. They even did silly things like standing in front of the magnificent fountains at the Bellagio and allowing the wind to blow the spray on them. Mary Ann and Edward, after the calls, however, sat down in their room for a serious conversation.

"You know what this means. The authorities and maybe even foreign agents will be here in days if not hours. Even if I alone speak with them, I don't know how to lie well enough to keep you safe. Edward what can we do?"

"Mary Ann, I knew this would happen. I hoped we could simply be with each other a little longer in Vegas but this probably will not be the case. If the agent called here, he will almost certainly find out where we are. I, of course, have a contingency plan. We'll buy a car through one of my corporations and head for my Montana house near Glacier

National Park. The home is magnificent. I've outfitted it with all the latest electronic equipment and its own generator. We can play music and broadcast it to the world with practically no risk of being traced or discovered. I have more than a year's worth of food in several walk in freezers and large dry cabinets. We can live there for a long time without any need of going anywhere."

"Sounds great, like an extended honeymoon."

"It will be. Of course, with a great deal of time on our hands, we can discuss what we really want to do with our lives. My objectives are to make music and to share my scientific knowledge with the world without affecting the balance of power among nations. If I can stay away from weapons development I can do that."

"I want to make music and help you. I think we will make a great team."

"We will. We will."

THE TRIP

The trip seemed to start well. The year old Chevy SUV owned by Wabash Inc., one of Edward's many shell corporations, waited for them in a lot on the outskirts of Las Vegas. They took a cab to the airport and then walked inside for a coffee. Minutes later, they loaded their bags in another cab and headed for the lot. After arriving at the lot, Edward provided the paperwork to the dealer, loaded their bags in the back and left. Yet, as they drove north toward Montana on route 95, the memory of a person in Vegas bothered both of them.

As they left the Venetian and headed down the Los Vegas strip, Mary Ann saw a man staring at them. The man made no gestures toward Mary Ann but followed their progress with his eyes. In a moment, he disappeared but his image did not. Mary Ann brought up the subject as the desert passed in their side windows.

"I saw a man staring at us. He looked like a cop. The man got a good look at me but not you. He probably saw your general outline. He seemed to recognize me. He may have been the private detective who came to the Homeless Pantry, I think his name is Rich but I don't remember him very well. As soon as he presented his credentials I looked away from him. The man may have seen us by chance or waited for us to drive past him. In either case, I think he will pursue us. If he is this detective he will definitely pursue us. I know that sounds paranoid, but I'm convinced of it."

"Mary Ann there is nothing paranoid about what you are saying. Many people are after me. Many of them are professionals. They know how to find people. We just have to stay ahead of them. I will trade this car in for another in Reno. I will also change the registration when and before we arrive in Montana. These simple steps will help. We haven't done anything wrong but the government will find ways to say that it is in the national interest to find and detain me. In any case, it will take time for them to discover how we left Las Vegas. They will think we left Vegas as most people do through the airport. We should be in another car by the time they discover what car we purchased from the Las Vegas dealer."

"As silly as this sounds, I feel a little like Bonnie and Clyde. The only difference is we haven't done anything wrong."

"What I have done wrong is to invent the most powerful weapons in the world, but at the same time made them difficult to copy or create. They control us and they control the weapons. Nothing will stop them coming for us." Edward responded.

Continuing their honeymoon, Edward and Mary Ann took a room at the Atlantis Casino Resort in Reno. After getting settled they headed to Better Odds Ford on the outskirts. Edward and Mary stared at the Sierra Nevada Mountains as they drove to the remote dealership. They talked about going to Lake Tahoe for a few days but knew they would not.

After they drove into the dealership, a florid man named Mike with a large belly and an equally large cowboy hat greeted them.

"Welcome to Better Odds Ford. How can I help you?"

"Well, I just bought this used Tahoe and I can't say I like it very much. I wondered whether you had an Explorer I could try with four wheel drive."

"I have a black dealer car. It has all the bells and whistles including four wheel drive. The owner drives it but he usually trades these cars away after he reaches two thousand miles. The odometer on this one says 2235. I can get you a good price. I'll show you the car while my used car manager takes a look at the Tahoe. You should have come to us first rather than our competitor."

"Yeah that sounds fine. Can my wife Sue and I drive it?"

"Sure I will get you the keys. By the way, Sue, do you dance in Reno at one of the casinos? If you don't I can hook you up with some of the people who hire beautiful women like you."

"No, Mike, I'm sorry I don't dance. My boyfriend and I are just driving through." Mary Ann replied.

"Oh I see, well here is the Explorer, what do you think?" Mike said.

"We like the looks. If it drives well, you have a sale." Edward said.

While Edward traded his Chevy Tahoe for a Ford Explorer, he placed the new car in another of his corporations Beamis Corp. After several days of first class service at their Vegas hotel, Edward and Mary Ann returned to the road. They headed for Boise, Idaho as their next destination on their way to the Glacier National Park area. Edward and Mary Ann saw many people staring at them but they couldn't tell why they did so. Mary Ann routinely attracted this kind of attention. She started wearing big sunglasses and a floppy hat to cover her appearance a little.

THE CHASERS

Back in his home office Rich stared at Rose for a long time and said.

"Rose will you marry me?"

"What, where did that come from? I've been waiting for you to say that for ten years. I must say that is not the most romantic way to pop the question but at least you did it. Why are you asking now?"

"Rose I've loved you for those ten years. I just never got around to asking. I have a hunch that Edward and Mary Ann went off to Los Vegas to marry. If we are going to Vegas for the case, we might as well do what we should have done ten years ago and join them."

"I've loved you from the beginning, but I wish you had asked differently. I suppose the only thing that really matters is that you asked. So the answer is yes of course I will marry you. When are we going to do this?"

"As soon as we can make arrangements. As to relatives, I hoped we could avoid all that. If you want to have a ceremony and party at some later date, I will play the role of the newlywed. But for now, I just want this marriage to be between the two of us."

"Alright, I'll start making some plans. And by the way, I want a ring and some other traditional things." Rose said.

"Oh I forgot. I have had this ring for some time." Rich said as he pulled a diamond engagement ring out of his drawer.'

"Rich you need some lessons on how to romance a lady and properly ask her to marry you, but you still have managed to make me a happy woman."

"I just wish I had asked you earlier. By the way, I want to leave as soon as possible. My inquiries may have tipped the couple off that I am after them. They won't wait in Vegas for me to come."

Hours later Rose and Rich headed for Las Vegas. But before they left for O'Hare Airport, Rich went to Mary Ann's high-rise with a warrant to search her condo. The big boxer reluctantly took Rich up to apartment and let Rich inside. The big man did, however, leave Rich with a warning.

"You have a legal right to search the apartment but if you mess it up, you will have me to deal with. When I boxed, I was known for my devastating right hook."

"I'll be careful", Rich said, after waving away the big black man. Rich spent almost forty-five minutes searching Mary Ann's condo. He found nothing of value. The condo looked almost too clean. Rich suspected that Mary Ann lived elsewhere but where he did not know. With time running out, he almost ran out of the high rise to pick up Rose for their trip to Vegas.

As soon as they checked into the Bellagio in Vegas, Rose and Rich went for a walk. Ten minutes into the walk, a car passed them with two figures Rich believed to be Edward and Mary Ann. He didn't have a good look at Edward but he saw Mary Ann clearly. Her beauty could not be well hidden. Rich knew it to be her the moment he saw her.

With barely a comment, Rich grabbed Rose and headed for the wedding mill they had chosen earlier, New Beginnings. Within an hour, Richard married Rose, checked out of the Bellagio and headed for the cab company, which operated the car where he saw Mary Ann. Rich and Rose never thought to ask the so-called pastor whether Edward and Mary Ann had been there earlier. Rich had also taken down the number of the cab. Rich should soon have the cab's destination.

Rose didn't accept this sudden change of plans lightly.

"That has to be one of the fastest weddings and honeymoons in history. I have a couple of poor quality I phone pictures to commemorate the event. Girls like me need a little more than that. I am asking myself why I fell in love with a detective."

"Rose I will make it up to you, I promise. I would have waited for our wedding but you started hinting about dating other men. You wanted to force my hand and you did. I wouldn't be able to function if you dated another man. Look, this is the biggest case I have ever had, a real game changer. It could make my reputation for life. By pure luck, I saw my targets. I can't let them slip away. I have to worry about our futures and yes of our children if we have any. I am a provider. So let me provide."

"It's my own fault. I pushed you and here is the result. But no matter how much I complain, I'm very happy right now. We're a team. We will have a regular wedding and honeymoon when the time is right." Rose said.

"Yes we will. The cab company headquarters is here. Let's see where our target's cab went."

Rich had a little difficulty persuading the clerk in the cab company to help him. His private detective license did not impress anyone. The letter the FBI provided him did. The letter, which he repeatedly produced and signed by the Deputy Director of the FBI asked all citizens to give Rich whatever help they could in his investigation. After the clerk read the letter, Rich spoke more forcibly the next time.

"Okay are you going to provide me with the information I need or am I going to ask the FBI to become involved"

"Okay I get it. Cab 1251 at 2:30 pm took a young couple to the airport. The cab driver was Mike. He should be in the break room. His shift begins in an hour and he likes to hang out for a little while before he leaves."

Rich saw a cab driver matching Mike's description munching a sandwich while he watched TV. Rich along with Rose approached the man. After introducing himself and showing Mike the letter, Mike responded.

"Yeah I remember them. In a city of gorgeous women, this woman stood out. I couldn't figure out how a nerdy looking guy could be dating this girl. Maybe he is one of those rich techy guys. We see a lot of them."

"Did they say where they were going?"

"No not really. They mentioned a flight but not where it headed. They talked a lot then all of a sudden they stopped talking. The babe said something about seeing a guy on the street. They seemed nervous and anxious at the end. They left me a nice tip and left. I can't really remember much else."

"There has to be more than that." Rose said.

"No not really. After you listen to the same conversations twenty or thirty times a day they all blend into each other. I play my radio pretty loud. I figure if they want to have private conversations, they should be able to do so without me listening to them. Still, I do hear bits of conversation." Mike said.

"Okay thanks Mike. If you can think of anything, here is my card. If I am right, the guy you picked up is an important scientist which we really need to find." Rich said.

"Yeah he looked like a scientist. Still, I can't figure out why that babe was with him."

When Rich and Rose left the taxi headquarters, they saw the beautiful Chinese girl watching them. Rich laughed.

"I'm glad we are doing the Chinese government's work for them. I think we need to leave some false leads for this intrepid lady. What do you think?"

"By all means, let's do that. I don't like someone else stealing our work." Rose replied.

Hours later, an exhausted Rose and Rich sat down in a lounge at the airport. They had checked every flight leaving Las Vegas around the time the young couple departed the cab at the airport and found no record of anyone like them on any flights leaving Los Vegas. No one even remembered seeing them. Suddenly, Rich threw his hands in the air.

"Of course, they never had any intention of flying anywhere. They merely came to the airport to throw us off the scent. Isaac and Mary Ann must have taken another cab or rented a car. We have new ground to plow."

"Yeah this is the non glorious part of this business, chasing after leads that go nowhere. Where should we start?"

"If they wanted to get out of town, they would probably just rent a car and leave. Let's check there first."

After checking all the rental agencies but having no luck, the couple returned to the airport. Rose said.

"Let's check the departure cab area. If we can find the person assigning cabs at this approximate time, he or she may remember something."

After showing the FBI letter to the airport officials overseeing this function, Rich and Rose acquired the name of the individual assigning cars a Nathan Remy. Nathan would be coming on the job in an hour. He had a cell phone but Rich determined based on his experience that asking Nathan in person would yield better results.

Forty-five minutes later, Nathan walked toward his station after leaving public transit. He walked slowly and deliberately. An official at the airport pointed him out to Rich and Rose. Rich approached him.

"Nathan my name is Richard. I'm a licensed private detective and a former Chicago Police Detective on assignment to the FBI. This is Rose my wife and assistant. I am looking for a scientist and his wife. Here is a picture of the wife, who is hard to forget and the scientist before he had plastic surgery. Do you remember assigning a cab to them at about 9 am this morning?"

"Nice to meet you Rich and of course your wife Rose. I don't remember the scientist very well but I sure remember the wife. What a babe! In a city of beautiful women she stands out. I put them in a cab at about this time. They wanted to go to a car lot but I can't remember which one. I have to ask so I can pair up passengers whenever possible. This place can become very crowded."

"Can you remember anything about the lot? Did it sell used cars, new cars, foreign cars, domestic cars?"

"I want to say it was a Chevy dealer but when you deal with hundreds of passengers in a shift it is hard to be certain."

While Nathan talked Rose hurriedly looked up Chevy dealers in the Los Vegas area. With seconds she started asking.

"Nathan is it /Ralph's, High Desert, Cowboy Mike's, Lucky Lucy's?" Rose said.

"I think Lucky Lucy's is it but I can't be sure. That is probably the best I can do." Nathan said.

"Okay we will go with that. Thanks Nathan. You have been helpful." Rich said.

For the next several hours, Rich and Rose checked out the various Chevy dealers in town, starting with Lucky Lucy's. They finally received a hit at Cowboy Mike's Chevrolet. The dealership had sold a dealer used Chevy Tahoe to a couple matching the description Rich and Rose gave them. The dealership registered the vehicle under the corporate name of Wild Blue. Neither the salesman nor the sales manager had any information as to where the couple headed. The couple had largely been silent on anything other than the transaction.

Moments after leaving the dealership, Rich contacted the FBI and asked them to put out an APB on the vehicle with the license plate, AR 45921. Without a word of protest, the FBI did so. Feeling somewhat positive about the day's work, Rich and Rose headed to their rental car. They would spend one more night at the Bellagio then head for wherever their car APB took them. As they moved into their car, they noticed the beautiful Chinese woman watching them. She had a habit of appearing at places and times, which seemed more than a little annoying. She would undoubtedly go into the dealership and ask the same questions as he did. Rich needed to discuss this problem with his FBI handlers.

A POWERFUL MEETING

In the bowels of the White House, President Walworth, his Defense Secretary, Conrad, Secretary of State, Lopez, CIA Director, Chen, FBI Director, Tipton, Science Advisor Rothschild, and Chief of Staff Thompson, met. The tension in the room could be strongly felt. Defense Secretary Conrad spoke.

"Director Chen and I have both verified what we are about to tell you. It is based on in person intelligence, paper documents and electronic mail intercepts. Many Americans risked their lives bringing it to you. What we are going to share with you is a plot to annihilate the U.S. and make Russia, China and North Korea the most powerful countries in the world.

"In 1961, the Russians detonated the most powerful nuclear weapon ever created in their arctic zone, the so called Tsar Bomba, RDS 220 with a yield of 50 megatons or 50 million tons of TNT. Russia made several of these weapons, which they stored in Siberia. During Russia's democracy period, an RDS 220 somehow made its way to North Korea. Apparently, an angry Russian General, who hated the degeneration of the Russian military, thought that North Korea might actually use the weapon rather than letting it rot in storage. This general disappeared into a labor camp and no one ever heard of him again but the damage had been done. In the years since, both the Russians and Chinese have tried to get the weapon back but with little success. North Korea has refused to acknowledge they have it. In any case, North Korea has not had the means to deliver the weapon and rightly fears the retaliation they would suffer if they were to deploy it. We have worried about this powerful weapon for years.

"At a recent secret meeting between these three countries in China, a plot right out of a Hollywood movie came into being. Russia would provide North Korea with their best missile a Topol M Ballistic Missile, which Russia would modify to carry their RDS 220 bomb. The Topol travels at 15,000 mph, evades incoming missiles and even releases decoys to prevent interception. It would be very hard to hit with our existing technology. The bomb would be aimed at Yellowstone National Park, which is in effect a Super Volcano. If this volcano were to explode, it would level everything within a radius of a thousand miles and plunge the world into a nuclear winter. Most of the U.S. and parts of Canada would be covered in volcanic ash. We would have problems continuing as a viable country. Crops throughout the world would fail. Billions of people would die of starvation. China would provide a hardened spent uranium shell to enable the RDS 220 to penetrate a hundred feet into the ground before detonating, thereby increasing the chances of the Yellowstone Super Volcano erupting.

"To prevent a retaliatory strike that China and Russia hope will be largely directed at North Korea, Russia and China will launch at the same time North Korea launches strikes on all our nuclear submarine and bomber based nuclear weapons. The super volcano would eliminate most of our ground based ICBMs. Under this scenario, North Korea, China and Russia have calculated their potential losses from our nuclear weapons and from the nuclear winter caused by the Yellowstone eruption and deemed it acceptable. These three countries have already constructed and provisioned vast underground bunkers to house their elites while their countries recover from the eruption and any of our nuclear devices that reach them. Presumably Europe would suffer similar devastation. They like us would be in no condition to fight Russia, China, and North Korea."

"We have interceptor missiles which can knock down many of the missiles aimed at us. We also have first generation laser guns that might knock down some more missiles. Yet, the effectiveness of these devices against the Topol according to our analysis only reaches 30%. We only have seconds to hit the Topol once it descends from the stratosphere.

We do, however, have very advanced lasers designed by Isaac, the great genius now hiding from us. They would easily destroy the Topol and all the other missiles fired by our enemies as well as any of their facilities but his laser systems require periodic adjustment. Because Isaac is angry about our militarization of his ideas, he has not adjusted them in a while. Isaac has also developed high-energy shields, which no weapon we are aware of can penetrate. As a result, we have deployed these shields on a few weapon systems. Isaac is currently missing after escaping our joint research facility with the Department of Energy located in Illinois. We are looking for him. We don't know how well Isaac's lasers work now but only how they did work. We can no longer afford to test them. The same is true with his shields. In fact, we believe the Chinese, Russians and North Korea are delaying their plans out of fear for what Isaac's weapons can do to their missiles and their other facilities. We expect they are looking for Isaac as hard as we are."

"Dick this is a pretty tall tale. Subjecting your own country to a nuclear winter does not make a lot of sense. Hundreds of millions of citizens will die in these three countries. Social order will break down. What leader of a country would try to do that?" The President replied.

"We know Kim in North Korea is crazy enough to do exactly that. We know that factions inside China and Russia are also crazy enough. While these factions in China and Russia probably wouldn't have enough power and control to implement this policy on their own, they don't need to do so. North Korea will do it for them. This week, we received intelligence that North Korea just received four of the modified Topol M missiles and their launchers. We have no idea who sent them only that they arrived. We also have grainy pictures of what looks to be the RS 220. Mr. President this threat is now more real than ever. Advisor Rothschild does this scenario and Isaac's part in it make sense to you? You know Isaac better than anyone." Secretary Conrad said.

"As to the Yellowstone Caldera, yes it has the capacity to do everything you say but there are many variables. Will the nuclear bomb set off an eruption? If it is an eruption will it be a partial or complete eruption? Finally, how much of the Caldera is in a molten eruptible state. Volcanic eruptions vary greatly in their explosive potential. In short, we do not know how bad the eruption will be. It could be localized, impact primarily the US and Canada or as you say have a worldwide impact. This may be a part of the Russian, North Korean and Chinese impact analysis. Being on the other side of the world, they may believe the super volcano will devastate their enemies but do little permanent damage to them. They could be right.

"As to Isaac or Edward as he calls himself now, I cannot explain his level of genius. In nature, we have many instances of genetic memory, where offspring without any experience somehow know exactly how to perform difficult tasks. Edward's ability to come up with different kinds of technology is amazing enough but what is even more amazing is that he makes the technology work with few if any mechanical changes. This could only occur if he built these amazing machines based on already proven technologies. Since these technologies don't exist on Earth and probably wouldn't exist for thousands of years, they must come from a genetic memory he has from an alien civilization. There is simply no other plausible explanation. What alien civilization this happens to be or how Edward has any memory of it, I don't know. His medical files show him to be a normal human but what he does is not normal in any way. We have of course tried to replicate his science but have had little success doing so. Much of his technology is based on three-dimensional mathematics, which seems to explain the quantum world in a way we don't understand. Edward has refused to teach anyone else this mathematics or how any of his technology works." Science Advisor Terry Rothschild said."

"Terry you seem to have a handle on this. Work with the rest of my advisors and cabinet to secure the scientist. Do whatever you have to do be it legal or illegal to make this happen. We will cover you here. We must have his technology to meet this threat." The President responded.

"Yes sir I will." The Science Advisor responded.

After a slight pause, the President continued. "Miguel what have North Korea, China, and Russian been telling you at state. I presume you have been informing them of our grave concern with these policies."

"Yes Mr. President we have. They of course dismiss such an attack as a fantasy, but I can tell the diplomats from these countries are as worried as we are. They oppose this craziness but are worried about their own safety. Powerful military leaders in both China and Russia strongly support this attack. We have information, passed on to us secretly by a frustrated foreign affairs officer, that Chinese technicians have appeared at the North Korea launch sites to help prepare the missiles. These technicians are well trained on both the RS 220 and the Topol M. Apparently, the Chinese have made improvements in both the bomb and the missile. This is a three country effort."

"Miguel I want you to increase pressure on the diplomats of these three countries, China and Russia directly and North Korea indirectly. Tell them if they don't respond we will start sending strategic bombers on missions near their borders. We have to make sure they understand that this attack will subject their countries to an all out nuclear attack from us. Tipton and Chen as I said before, you need to work with Terry to find this scientist. We need to be able to blast their missiles out of the sky at a much higher level of certainty than 30%. These three countries may be just posturing but we can't afford to take any chances. Also, Conrad I want you to research just how much of our nuclear deterrent would be wiped out by this plot and to make the necessary changes to improve our retaliatory capability. Finally, I want to know how likely it is that this missile strike will trigger the Yellowstone super volcano." The President said.

"Mr. President we are already researching these questions. Our best geologists and volcanologists think this missile if it penetrates deeply enough could trigger the super volcano. We are also increasing our surveillance of North Korea and our capabilities against them. This threat will not go unchallenged." Secretary Conrad said.

"Okay. I may have to go public on this plot at some point, but before I do, I want every effort made to counteract it. Gentlemen, you all have your assignments. Get working." The President said as he rose and left the situation room.

BEAUTIFUL MOUNTAINS

The trip from Reno through Boise and mainly north from there seemed to pass with little effort. The scenery captivated both Mary Ann and Edward and caused them to spend a great deal of time in their own thoughts, staring out the side or front window. They played music that they felt enhanced the beautiful countryside they passed. The couple tried not to think of the considerable challenges they faced. Edward brought some extra sets of car plates and frequently changed those on the explorer as just one more precaution. When he did, Edward made the necessary computer changes to the DMV records in several states. Several times state highway police looked at the SUV but made no further inquiry when the plates didn't match those on their alerts. Still, Edward and Mary Ann felt the pressure each time a policeman examined their car. Edward joked that they had become human chameleons.

They stayed along the road north of Boise. The Boise area hotel sold itself as the Lariat. The Lariat had very little in the way of amenities but nonetheless seemed to be clean and well kept. The Lariat had one of those massage beds activated by a quarter. Mary Ann and Edward enjoyed using the feature in a number of funny ways as they used up all their quarters. The next morning, they drove northeast through Whitefish on the way to their spectacular home bordering Glacier National Park. They thought about spending some time on or near Sanders Lake but in the end just kept moving. In fact, they could have stopped a hundred places along the way but knew that the longer they stayed anywhere the greater danger they faced of being discovered.

Edward purchased their contemporary stone and glass home on a cliff overlooking Glacier National Park on the Internet. He studied the many videos e-mailed to him and arranged for workers to clean and maintain the large home. He also had a number of renovations done to the home. The 25,000 square foot house, dug into the solid rock of the cliff, sported two levels. The large master bedroom occupied the second level with a direct view eastward and the even larger combination living room and dinning room occupied the floor underneath it. The views could only be described as a stunning with the mountains of Glacier Park in the distance. The home had a large kitchen, 8 bathrooms, several with Jacuzzi tubs, a recreation room, a large laboratory at the back of the home with every kind of equipment imaginable, an indoor swimming pool, a broadcast and performance room and four additional bedrooms. Massive freezers, refrigerators and dry closets had enough food to feed them for two years.

Beneath the home stairs led to a natural cavern in the cliff, which the previous owner expanded to allow his helicopter and ultra light aircraft to take off and land. To make sure that the cavern did not compromise the integrity of the cliff, the previous owner installed massive concrete support columns. As an engineer the previous owner had the entire house wired for sound and video. A large satellite dish on the grounds provided the connection to the outside world.

The previous owner had reportedly spent $20 million on the home but after he died his heirs sold it for a much smaller amount to Edward. Edward spent an additional two million on the home primarily on the broadcast room and his laboratory. Edward desperately wanted to visit the home but had refrained, wanting Mary Ann to see it with him for the first time. They both spent an entire hour walking through the home and trying to visualize how they would live there. Finally, they both stood in front of the large picture window downstairs looking at the view. Edward spoke.

"First, I am going to install an impenetrable high energy shield surrounding the property. I already had the components sent here before we arrived. I have little fear of the potentially dangerous cougars, bears, snakes and wolves that frequent this area but I do fear warriors from ours and other governments attacking us. This shield should protect us from these threats. If the attack becomes too ferocious, we can always escape with our helicopter or ultra light plane in the hangar below. Although not an expert, I'm certified on both of these aircraft. As a younger man, I loved flying. The home also has cameras and sensors spread throughout the woods and along the access road. We will know if anything comes for us. I hope we evaded everyone, but our dogged hunters may still find us. Despite these problems, I think we can be happy here for some time."

"I'm happy. I intend to start a novel while you work in your laboratory and then we as a team can make music. For now, that is all I need. If our pursuers come for us, we can deal with the problem when it arises. I'm not going to live my life in fear."

"Sounds perfect to me. The world can do without my science for now." Edward replied taking Mary Ann into his arms.

THE FRUSTRATING PURSUIT

Rich and Rose stalled in Reno. They tracked down the car dealer who sold Mary Ann and Edward their Ford Explorer but had difficulty identifying the plates being used. They spent countless hours in the DMV files of many states looking for the vehicle. When they finally found the most current registration four precious days had passed. Wherever Mary Ann and Edward journeyed they had undoubtedly reached their destination. They could be anywhere. Over these four days, they saw the beautiful Chinese girl several times; then they didn't see her anymore. Rich vented his frustration.

"Do you think the Chinese girl has a lead? We haven't seen her for at least a day. I should have staked out her hotel. I asked the FBI about her. They think she is a Chinese spy but they don't have any substantial proof. She is a US citizen. China has a new program where they use leverage to convert Chinese Americans into spies. Her father is an importer of Chinese goods. Chinese officials could easily ruin the father if they so chose to do so. The FBI thinks that this is how they converted her. They want me to monitor her closely, but they don't want to pick her up. If they do, the Chinese will simply substitute someone else. This person could be harder to track. The devil you know is better than the one you don't."

"Rich she probably has the same type of resources we do. It's possible she has information on a siting of the SUV. We should track her for a change. Let's find out whether she checked out of her hotel and if so when." Rose said.

"A good idea. I saw her turn into a holiday inn. We can start our search there."

Susan Wang took a different approach. She followed Rich and Rose to Reno but soon realized that they were stuck. So she hauled out a map of the West and began to study it. She traced several routes to remote places in the West. Susan managed to identify ten possible routes to different remote areas. Susan then based on what the car dealer told her determined when May Ann and Edward/Isaac left Reno and where in a day of travel they might be. She then identified all the modest hotels on the different routes where Mary Ann and Edward might have stopped. She compiled a list of two hundred hotels on the different routes and began to call each of them. She had one big advantage. Susan knew the clerks/owners would remember a very beautiful young woman with a man who looked like a scientist. Susan became very frustrated. Most of the hotels and motels she called genuinely wanted to help her, but many did not want to speak with her or cooperate. One even checked her identity with the FBI and returned a call to her with threats. Susan had to throw away one of her burner phones and quickly leave the area she had taken rooms.

Refusing to be discouraged, Susan began to visit some of the hotels and motels where the owners had not been helpful. Months passed but Susan persisted. Her Chinese handlers gave her no choice. Finally, five long months after she lost Mary Ann and Edward, an exhausted Susan drove into the Lariat Motel. The owner eyed her suspiciously but gave her a room anyway. The Lariat had a small restaurant. Susan after unpacking some things sat down to eat a small semi tough filet, some mashed potatoes and over cooked string beans, covered with a thick sauce. The sauce, which did not look very good actually made the whole meal tolerable. Susan struck up a conversation with the waitress Betty who just happened to be the owners' daughter. After gaining the woman's trust, Susan showed Betty her fake FBI badge and began to ask some serious questions.

"Betty a very important scientist, who is critical to our national defense, has disappeared. We desperately need to find him. We believe he is travelling with a beautiful young woman, who he may have married in Las Vegas under an assumed name. Have you seen anyone like this?"

"Well ordinarily we don't share information like this with anyone. My dad Chuck is a privacy nut. He doesn't like answering government questions. Still, we are a patriotic family. My dad is an army veteran who fought in Vietnam. I'm not sure what I should say. Oh okay I guess it's all right. I do remember a couple like that. They stayed here about five months ago. Ordinarily I wouldn't remember somebody from that long ago, hundreds of people have stayed here since then, but the woman looked like she just walked off the pages of my fashion magazines. I have never seen a woman that beautiful before. And just like you said, the guy with her looked like a scientist. He seemed nice. You could tell he was really smart by the way he looked. They only stayed one night. They ate where you are eating now."

"Did you talk to them? Did they indicate where they were headed?"

"No not really. They didn't want to talk to me. But I think I heard them talking about the road to the North. This would make sense. Most of the people that come through here are on their way to Glacier National Park. I can see why. It is very beautiful there."

"Did you see the car they were driving?' Susan asked.

"No I didn't but dad always writes down the cars people park here. He doesn't like strange cars in our lot. He calls the police."

After eating her dinner, Susan went to the front desk to talk with Chuck. She felt very anxious about talking with the man. The way Chuck looked at her made Susan feel uneasy, but Susan absolutely had to know what kind of car Edward and Mary Ann drove. She approached Chuck with a smile.

"When I checked in, I didn't tell you everything about me. I am an FBI agent hunting for a very important scientist. Here is my identification."

Susan handed over the identification with some confidence. The Chinese forgers who made it were among the best in the world at their craft. No ordinary man would be able to tell the difference. Chuck stared at the ID for a long time and then finally said.

"Okay the ID looks legitimate. What can I help you with?"

"Your daughter said she saw this scientist and his beautiful wife about 5 months ago. She thought they were headed north. Do you happen to remember what kind of car they drove?"

"I record the make and color of all the cars that come here, but I only keep the information for two months. Then I delete it. I do remember the couple, but unfortunately, I can't remember what car they drove after all this time. I can't really add to what my daughter already told you. Sorry about that."

"It's okay. You and you're daughter have already been helpful. I'll be checking out early tomorrow, probably around 6. Will you be here?"

"Yeah, I should be at the desk then? A lot of the people who stay here check out around then. By the way, you aren't Vietnamese are you? I'm a Vietnam vet. I lost a lot of friends to the Vietcong during that war." Chuck answered.

"No I'm of Chinese heritage but I grew up here. My Mandarin and Cantonese are terrible. I couldn't make it in China and don't know that much about the place."

"You folks look all the same to me. My Korean War Vet friends saw plenty of you Chinese. You were worse than the Vietnamese. Anyway, I got to check on a water problem in the basement. See you tomorrow."

Susan nervously left the front desk. She might even leave this place before 6 am tomorrow. The hostility in Chuck's eyes truly frightened her.

Chuck didn't have a water problem. He had fixed a leak the previous week. Instead he called the local FBI office and asked if the FBI had an agent named Susan Collingsworth working for them. The owner of the Lariat became suspicious about the call they received from the Chinese lady. She identified herself as an FBI agent but the owners to be sure called the local office and told them of the call. They had never heard of a Susan Collingsworth. Ten minutes after the call, the FBI called back and said that the information they provided to this impostor involved national security. A detective named Rich and his new wife Rose would be driving to their hotel. They were asked to talk with them and only them about what they knew.

Rich and Rose, who had by this time returned to Chicago, caught a flight to Boise and upon deplaning, quickly grabbed a rental car waiting for them. Rich complained very bitterly about the information they received from the Lariat owners through the FBI.

"Its embarrassing. We look like dopes. I'm surprised the FBI didn't fire us. We have spent the last several months trying every trick we know to find the scientist and in the end this call gave us the information we should have developed on our own. How did the Chinese girl figure out where Isaac and Mary Ann headed? We received no information like this from our contacts."

"Rich you know our business better than I. Sometimes people get lucky or try an approach we did not. We just need to catch up with our Chinese friend. One thing that bothers me is what happens if our Chinese adversary finds Mary Ann and Edward at the same time or before we do. What do the Chinese do with the information? They will probably try to kidnap the couple. We would of course try to stop the Chinese but if we tried to do so it could be very dangerous for us."

"Then we better make sure we get to the couple first. We just need to do our job this time. I don't want us involved in an international incident."

An hour after landing, Rose and Rich pulled into the Lariat. Rich broke more than a few speed records on the short drive. Bud the man behind the counter quickly extended his hand and began talking quickly.

"Are you Rich and Rose? The FBI told me you would be coming."

"Yes we are. We're trying to find out some information on a young couple who stayed here."

"You're not the only one. A Chinese girl came by here looking for the young couple. She said they were friends and that they told her they would be staying at my hotel. That's a lie. Even though she denied it, the girl called me on the phone earlier and asked about the couple. She claimed to be an FBI agent on the phone but when I called the FBI they had no record of someone like her working for the FBI. I fought in the Vietnamese War. The Vietnamese almost killed me. Some of my friends at the VFW said the same thing happened to them in the Korean War. She's a Chinese spy, no doubt about it. I pulled out my shotgun when she checked out in the morning. I'd a killed her or held her for you but the FBI told me to let her go. Whatever that young couple is into it sure must be a big deal for a foreign nation and the FBI to be involved. By the way my name is Chuck, Chuck Wallworth."

"Thank you Chuck. Yeah the FBI told me the same thing about the Chinese girl. They want a spy they know and can follow, not one they don't. Do you know anything more about this couple?"

"As a matter of fact I do. We provide a little food service for our guests, nothing fancy but some basic food. The young couple ate a little at our restaurant before they went to bed. Without looking too obvious, we tried to overhear what they were saying. I turned my hearing aid up to maximum. I didn't get anything but my daughter who serves as a waitress thought she heard them they say they were headed North into Western Montana. One of the most beautiful spots in this country Glacier National Park is up that way. If I had to guess, they would be headed there. Also, I have the make, color and license plate of the SUV they were driving. Ordinarily I don't keep that information passed two months but I have a special box I throw this information into if the guests look shady or suspicious. I keep this information for a year." Bud said.

"Thanks Bud, we can use that information, especially the SUV identification. We will head the same way that the scientist and his wife headed. We will leave early tomorrow morning. It is helpful to us in law enforcement when citizens like you step forward." Rich said.

"Glad to help. I'm a loyal citizen. I didn't stop serving my country when I left the army." Chuck said with pride.

After Chuck left, Rose said.

"He is guessing, but his guess is better than what we have."

"Yeah I agree, but if he is right, the area near the park is vast. We need a way to pin it down. I say we find the town nearest to the park and look for a realtor there. They should know the houses in the area. Edward would want a special house where he could be secluded but at the same time do his research. A small cabin would not do. He certainly can afford it. No one knows how rich he is. The government can't find his accounts. Yet from his income taxes, it would appear that Edward is worth as much as $50 mm with a large income every month. With that kind of money he can buy whatever he wants. Also, I will run the plates of his SUV and see if any businesses up that way might have recorded his vehicle." Rich added.

"Yeah that ought to work pretty well, but I have a bad feeling about all this. We could be way out of our league. The Chinese could send in their Special Forces to kidnap the scientist. We wouldn't stand a chance against them." Rose worried.

"That is why we are going to locate the scientist and the girl, tell the FBI and get the heck out of this part of the country. Who knows how many armed men will show up looking for this scientist."

"Amen to that." Rose laughed.

CONVERGENCE

Susan's entire body shook with fear. The owner of the Lariat intended to kill her. Susan saw it in his eyes. Susan would have to be more careful of the disguises and impersonations she undertook in the future. Susan assumed the FBI told this so called patriot not to shoot or detain her. Why they did so remained a mystery. Perhaps they felt more comfortable with a Chinese agent they knew than one they did not. A guy she once dated, a former Special Forces soldier, had the same look in his eyes as the Lariat owner. Because of the look, Susan had broken off their relationship. Susan polished off a half of bottle of wine before she could finally gain control of her fears and stop the shaking of her limbs. Susan still had a job to do. She decided to revert back to her follow the detectives' strategy. The owners of the Lariat knew something, which they had undoubtedly shared with Rich and Rose. They would follow up on what the Lariat owners told them. Susan would simply follow them. Still, for the first time, Susan realized that all her clever disguises and moves hadn't been so clever after all. The US government probably knew what she did for the Chinese government. Susan now had no home. She betrayed her country. The government would surely imprison her as a spy when they had no further use for her. As she pursued the scientist, Susan would have to find a way to leave this country. Her life and freedom depended upon it.

Although troubled, Susan enjoyed the beautiful ride toward Western Montana. Following her earlier pattern, she switched her rental car to a small Kia in place of the Chevrolet she drove earlier. With a ball cap hiding her beautiful long hair and loose wrinkled clothes she could not be easily recognized. Rich and Rose, when Susan fell in line behind them, gave no indication that they recognized her. She followed them for hours.

Under the assumption that Rose and Rich traveled to the Glacier National Park Area, Susan had already examined all the realtors selling expensive residences in the vast area. One stood out from the rest. Big Sky Realtors located in Whitefish. Susan had already called and made an appointment with Janet the owner of Big Sky, as a wealthy Californian seeking an unusual and outstanding home in the area. If Rose and Rich headed in a different direction, Susan would call and cancel but she had a strong feeling that Rich and Rose headed to the Glacier National Park Area.

Meanwhile Rose and Rich followed a similar path. They had appointments to see the same woman in Big Sky an hour after Susan but also had added Elk Horn Realtor to their list. Despite their plan, Rich and Rose realized they had no confirmation that Edward and Mary Ann traveled to this area or that if they did whether they had purchased a home. They might be renting or just staying in a resort or hotel. Lady luck would be needed to find this couple. So far, no person or camera had caught Edward and Mary Ann's SUV. They didn't have as many cameras or people in this rural area as they had in a city.

Susan spent a considerable amount of time dressing in her best clothes and jewelry for her realtor meeting. She needed to convince the woman at Big Sky that she commanded both power and money and thus could represent a major sale. Information would flow freely in such a case.

Janet, a smartly dressed woman with expensive cowboy boots to add a little western flare, eyed Susan carefully. She knew the San Francisco area where this woman allegedly came had many wealthy Asian Americans. For this reason, Janet slowly formed a smile. This woman looked like the real deal. She extended her hand and began speaking.

"Susan is it. I'm Janet. Welcome to the most beautiful corner of America. Many Californians come here looking for a little space. I have ranches, vacation homes, condos, You name I have it. What is your preference?"

"Actually, I am looking for one of a kind type home with spectacular views and a great deal of privacy. Money is no object."

"I have many homes like that. Let me bring the book. I have the material on line but I find people prefer looking at old fashioned pictures if they can." Janet said.

Janet and Susan spent the next half hour looking at homes. Susan kept shaking her head. Finally, Susan said with some pretended exasperation.

"I'm sorry these homes just aren't making it. Do you have any homes that might be for sale or ones that sold recently to a buyer who hasn't used them? I'd be willing to pay a premium for the right house."

"Well there was one house. I sold the original owner the property, a one of a kind piece that bordered the Glacier National Park. The property included a rock ledge that provided a spectacular view of the park. The property should have been part of the park but for a number of complex reasons it remained in private hands. The original owner reportedly built a stunning home on this property. By the time he finished, this owner had plowed upward of $40 mm into the place. I spent a tremendous amount of time and effort trying to sell the place even though the property had an open listing. When the original owner died, the kids who inherited the home didn't believe in exclusive listings. A buyer bought it on line for about $21 million. I didn't get a penny out of it. No one around here has even seen this buyer. I looked up the deed and it is registered to a private closely held corporation. I am not even sure who to approach about buying it." Janet said.

"The property sounds perfect. Do you have any pictures? Can you tell me where it is? I'd be willing to pay you for your efforts." Susan said with some enthusiasm.

"Since I sold their dad the original piece of property they did send me a number of pictures of it online. I don't think you could find it online any longer. The new owner deleted all pictures of it as soon as he closed. As to the location, we have a longitude and latitude heading. At least five miles of the road up there isn't paved. You would need a four wheel drive truck to access the place." Janet said slowly.

"I tell you what. I will give you a $1000 to look at the pictures and another $1000 to show me up there if I like it. Of course, if I am able to buy the property, I will give you a realtor's percentage for helping me, say 6%. How does that sound?

"Great I'll bring the pictures up on the computer." Janet responded as Susan slipped her ten one hundred dollar bills. Susan kept large amounts of money provided by the Chinese government in case she needed to pry information from people.

Susan eagerly scanned the pictures provided by Janet. From the first picture, she knew that this would be the house Edward and Mary Ann would purchase. The fact that they purchased it on line and wanted to keep their identity secret just reinforced her suspicions. Without a moment's hesitation, she said.

"Janet this is it, the house of my dreams. To be absolutely sure, I would like to go up there. Maybe the owner will be there. I can make him an offer on the spot. Would you be willing to take me?"

"Yes we will go tomorrow at say 9 am. It will take a couple of hours to get there. The terrain can be difficult. Until then, I will give you the coordinates. You can use them to get a better lay of the land around the place. You might be able to see it on Google maps." Janet added.

"Thanks. I would appreciate that very much."

Hours later, Susan spoke with her Chinese handler.

"I've sent you pictures and location coordinates of a house that would fit the needs of Edward in the Glacier National Park Area. If Edward bought a house, this would be it. I have absolutely no doubts about that. Still, I have no confirmation that he bought a house up here only that he and his wife came this way. Janet the local realtor and I will head up there tomorrow so I can try and obtain some confirmation of my theory. The place has a security fence and locked gate. If anyone is home, they probably won't let me inside. Also, the FBI consultants are hot on my heels. If I found this place so will they. Unless we act quickly, I can't guarantee our extraction team will get there first. In essence, to beat the competition we have to gamble, but I don't know if we have enough information to do so."

"We will position our spy satellites to get a better look. Depending on what we see, we will send the extraction team. I want you to go up there as planned. There is nothing like actually being there. The moment you gain any information that confirms your theory contact me. This assignment carries the highest priority of any that I have ever seen. Our lives and our fortunes may very well depend on its outcome."

"I will do as you ask." Susan said.

The next day Susan marveled at the great beauty of the area. Janet drove on increasingly smaller and rougher roads until the pavement disappeared altogether. Janet's four-wheel drive Jeep Wagoneer transferred the bounces with more and more authority. A cloud of dust formed behind them. Finally, after 30 minutes of this uncomfortable jostling, a road appeared on the left. Janet without hesitation turned down the narrow road. The magnificent house perched on the cliff appeared suddenly and Janet screeched to a stop in front of the gate. The house lights shone in a very strange way. They seemed to glisten and shimmer. Both Janet and Susan left the car and approached the squawk box next to the gate. Janet spoke authoritatively into the box.

"This is Janet of Big Sky realty in Whitefish. I have a buyer who badly wants to buy your house. Name your price and this wealthy buyer will pay it. Offer like this don't come along everyday." Janet said.

Second later, the box came to life. "I'm sorry but we have no interest in selling. We have all the money we need. Whatever your offer is it will not be attractive to us. Now please leave. We will not respond to you again."

Janet whispered $50 mmm and Susan nodded. "How does $60 mm sound? That is double what it is worth." Silence followed Janet's statement. She tried again. "How about $80 mm?" Silence followed again. Shaking her head. Janet said. "I'm sorry Susan, the buyer just isn't interested."

Meanwhile, Susan grabbed a long stick and walked along the fence to the left of the gate. She kept walking until she had gone far enough to be out of hearing distance. Then Susan poked the fence with her stick. The stick stopped in mid air and began burning. Susan picked up a rock and threw it at a space above the fence. The rock bounced off the invisible wall and landed near Susan's feet. The rock glowed. Susan immediately dialed her cell phone and said simply when her handler answered.

"This is the scientist's place. There can be no doubt about it."

"Leave, Our team is on the way."

Meanwhile, Janet called Rich and Rose who had visited her after Susan. "This is the house, no doubt about it and the scientist seems to have answered our call. You'd better hurry. Your Chinese spy just called someone after testing what must be an energy shield. I doubt she called the hairdresser."

"Leave now Janet. We're calling the cavalry. It might become a little dicey up there. And as we said before leave the Chinese spy to us."

"Okay but as a western gal I sure would like to see the battle that comes. I'm waving to the spy now. I knew she was a fake as soon as I raised the price to $80mm. No way anyone is going to pay that kind of money for this house."

Janet hung up and waved to Susan who walked toward her with a smile on her face. 5 minutes later they drove back down the bumpy road that took them to the house.

ROAD TRIP

Mary Ann and Edward had spent many months at their Montana home when Mary Ann suddenly said.

"Edward the winter is coming very soon. Once we have the first big snowfall we will be snowed into this place. Before that happens, I want to do something a little crazy. I want to go to Spokane and perform at the Lazy Daisy Susan a little bar that caters to artists like us. I think it will be fun. Anyway, if our pursuers are hot on our heels, this sudden trip will throw them off the scent."

"You may have something there. I can rig the answering system at the house to my phone. I can talk to anyone from the government as if we were both in the house. I can also arm my new high-energy shield. Unless they bring a whole army, they won't be able to gain access to the house. If they do get inside, I will self destruct all my important science projects like the shield. Even better, if they do this, I can broadcast their illegal search to the entire world on the Internet."

"Sounds great. I suppose we will be somewhat exposed on our way to and from Spokane and while we are there, but we have to assume some risk. Whatever we do will expose us." Mary Ann replied.

"Not as much as you might think. I have finalized my first two personal protective shields. No weapon we know of should be able to penetrate them. We will be free of most risks. They can detect both poisonous gas and poison in food and drink. They can even be made to shock someone trying to grab us. The shields are invisible but do lend a little sheen to our images. If our pursuers find us, we will simply refuse to go with them."

"Sounds great. I will pack immediately." Mary Ann said as she walked to their bedroom.

Many hours later, Mary Ann and Edward journeyed west toward Spokane on Interstate 90. They just crossed the border into Idaho. Edward tied the navigation screen into the video feed from the house. They listened to old folk rock from the 70's. They rolled down the windows to absorb the clean fresh air. They smiled a lot and sang to the music on the radio. Mary Ann commented.

"Edward your singing voice is not half bad, certainly good enough to sing background. You are on key and your rhythm is good. You'll never be a lead vocalist but your blending well with me."

"Yeah I seem to blend with you Mary Ann on many different levels. Oh wait a minute. A car is driving up to our house. I can see it on our monitor. Who on earth could they be? The driver looks familiar but the pretty Chinese woman I have never seen before. They are contacting us through the intercom. I will say very little to them. I see no benefit in doing so particularly since we are not there."

After the exchange, which consisted of the two women repeatedly asking to speak with Edward, Edward turned off the verbal feed and spoke to Mary Ann.

"They both made phone calls after they tried to speak with us. I can't make out what they said but if I had to guess they called in the cavalry. They want access to our house and to us. Since they each made calls, they may have called in different groups. The Chinese woman may work for the Chinese government. In any case, this should become very interesting. I think we are going to have a show to watch on our way to Spokane.'

"Edward that is a frightening thought. I'm glad we are not there. I'd be scared to death." Mary Ann replied.

"I'm going to put the whole show on the Internet. If the government does anything illegal, I want the whole country to see it. One good thing about this show is that it will divert attention away from us in Spokane. They will be looking for us in Montana."

"Yes that is a blessing. We are going to do our very first gig together if you don't count that time with Slim. I think it will be great."

"So do I honey so do I?"

THE BATTLE

David Hua stared at his hardened Special Forces team with more than a little pride. The rented surplus US army helicopter while not a first line unit, worked well enough. They had already programmed the navigation to send them to Montana home of the American Scientist. Despite the readiness of his team to kidnap the American Scientist from his home, doubts nagged at the squad leader.

According to his intelligence briefing, the American Scientist's home would be protected by an impenetrable shield. David possessed the latest generation offensive laser produced by Chinese scientists and the most powerful conventional explosive known to man but he did not know how they would affect this shield if indeed the shield even existed. David did not like dealing with what seemed to him like science fiction. David even had some high tech drilling equipment to burrow under the shield but he did not know whether this would work either. Finally, whatever device or devices he had to use to gain access to the house would take time to use. Even if he were first to arrive on the scene others would follow, including the Americans who after all controlled the area. Oh and just prior to lift off, reports of a spy within his own ranks might have conveyed the location of the scientist's house to other foreign countries came into his possession. This spy had apparently been handled but David and his team had no way to prepare for an all out war against other forces like his own.

An hour later David and his crew landed in a clearing on the edge of the scientist's property. With superb training and precision, Hua's team quickly assembled their equipment and took it to what seemed to be a perimeter area. Hua could clearly see a shimmering effect on the fence surrounding the property, which he assumed to be a shield. He turned to his second in command Jin.

"Take that large rock in front of you and throw it at the shimmering shield in front of you."

Jin motioned one of the other members of the team to come forward and together they lifted and threw the rock at the shield. The rock bounced off the shield as if it had hit a brick wall.

"There is certainly some kind of shield present. Jin set the charges."

Jin along with the rest of the team quickly placed charges at the base of the shimmering shield and joined David behind a rock cover 10 meters away. Jin detonated the charge and a powerful shock wave came back toward them. When the dust cleared, the shield displayed no ill effects. It remained as before.

"Assemble the ray gun. This should provide the punch we need to penetrate the shield." David said without a moment's hesitation.

Ten minutes later the ray gun pointed right at the area where the charges detonated. Jin stood quietly at the controls waiting for David to speak.

"This shield could be dangerous. Jin when the rest of us take cover in the same area as before fire the gun at will. Of course you need to take cover before you do."

"Yes sir. Moments later with the rest of the team safely hidden, Jin fired the gun, but failed to provide himself enough cover. A powerful surge of energy erupted from the gun but upon hitting the shield reflected back toward Jin, destroying him and the gun in a brilliant flash of light. Once again, the shield showed no ill effects. Undaunted, David spoke again.

"We will have time to mourn the loss of Jin later. Bring out the digging machine and commence the construction of a tunnel underneath the shield."

Without comment, the remaining five members of the team did as asked. Within twenty minutes they had a crawling tunnel to the shield six feet underneath the ground. The men quickly crawled through the tunnel to the shield area but to their surprise they confronted the same shimmering shield. Doug Lee spoke.

"Leader, the shield is as strong under ground as it is above ground. There is no access here."

David stood for a moment in silence deciding what to do next when he heard a loud rumbling sound coming up the drive. A large truck followed by several cars drove toward the gate to the property. The driver who looked Russian to Hua dove out of the lead truck and rolled into the bush. David ordered his men to dive toward the ground as well, putting his hands over his ears as he did so. The truck filled with explosives hit the gate and detonated into a huge fireball. Debris flew everywhere. The shock wave damaged the Chinese team's ears despite their hands being tightly secured over their ears. A huge hole formed in the ground, but the shield remained as it was before. The explosion had no impact.

Despite Hua's disinterest in the Russian team, their leader yelled at him in heavily accented English.

"This is a Russian Special Forces Operation. I suggest you leave if you want to remain safe."

"Your threats are meaningless to me. My men and I are very well trained and armed. We have our mission too but if the truth be told neither one of us have any way of penetrating the shield surrounding this property."

"You're wrong. As we speak, I have part of my team climbing the cliff behind us. There is a wide opening the previous owner used as place to land his helicopter and ultra light aircraft. We will gain access there."

"No you won't. We are of course aware of this entrance. It is clearly visible on our satellite images. The problem is the same shield that stops us here also encloses the entrance to the cavern in the cliff. You're men will have no where to go when they reach this area."

"We will see about that. I'm warning you a second time to leave here. This is a Russian operation."

"We are leaving but not because of you. I just received a notice on my phone. A massive American force is on their way up here. They won't like a foreign force trying to take their scientist. We have a much better chance of escaping here in our helicopter than you do on the ground. Until, we see each other again." Hua said as he motioned his forces back to the waiting helicopter.

As Hua's helicopter took off, the American Force arrived by helicopter and road. The Russians greeted the Americans with machine gun fire but an Apache Helicopter obliterated them with Gattling Gun fire. The Americans ignored the Chinese force. One international incident seemed to be more than enough for the American Army. They only engaged the direct threat in front of them.

GENERAL PORTER

Square jawed and built like the All American Wrestler he used to be, General Porter, his Ranger badges attached to his chest, watched the Russian Special Forces fall in a hail of bullets with a look of indifference on his face. The other Russians climbing the cliff had fallen as well from their perches on the mountainside after being intercepted by the Apache. Butch Porter wanted to mow down the Chinese Special Forces departing as he arrived but his superiors ordered him to let them go. The Army Brass apparently could handle only one international incident at a time. Butch didn't care about things like that. Butch regarded these Foreigners as invaders and would have gladly put a bullet in their heads himself. Butch a man of action did not dwell on these thoughts for long. He had a mission, capture the American Scientist and his girlfriend. If they can't be captured, kill them so opposing nations cannot capture and use the great scientist.

He would accomplish this mission no matter what it took. Butch had even ignored the FBI who allegedly participated with him in a joint operation. He had taken the four FBI men and placed them with a guard detail in the back of his task force. To avoid unnecessary complications, he had removed their communication devices and weapons. When they had not complied with his orders willingly, the General handcuffed them. General Butler had no use for civilian cheap suits. They would get all the credit for this operation but they would have no hand in it.

The army general approached the front gate and without hesitation jumped in the six-foot hole now in front of it. He had to yell up to the house microphone, which showed no damage from its position behind the shield.

"This is Army General Butch Porter. Open this gate at once or suffer the consequences. You have five minutes to respond or I will attack your home with the might and force of the US Army. I have orders to capture you dead or alive."

The small speaker next to the microphone crackled to life.

"This is Edward owner of this home. Where is your search warrant?"

"I have no warrant, just orders from the President of the U.S."

"Then you have no right to enter my home. The constitution trumps the will of the armed forces and even the President any day of the week."

"I don't care about your warrants. The JAG officer assigned to me can worry about this when the time comes. Either open this gate or I will blow this house off the map. This is a matter of National Security."

"Without a warrant I will not open the gate period. My lawyers are already in federal court protesting your actions here."

General Porter shook his head, climbed out of the hole in front of the gate, and then walked back to his bunker, which had been established 100 meters away. The General then barked out "fire" over his intercom. The General would not wait for a warrant and all the complications that would come with it.

What happened next truly astounded all those in a position to witness it including the millions of people on the Internet Edward had included in the spectacle. His multitude of cameras, securely behind the shield, caught they entire thing. Literally hundreds of bombs, missiles, howitzer shells, rockets and small arms fire rained down on Edward's shield guarding his house. The sound, the fire, smoke literally overwhelmed the senses. As a grand finale three cruise missiles crashed into the shield and detonated. The area outside the shield, an attractive forest of magnificent pines, spruces and aspens, became a virtual wasteland.

When the smoke cleared and the fires began to die, General Porter climbed out of his bunker and removed his heavy ear phones designed to protect his ears and walked slowly toward Edward's home. To his astonishment, the shield looked exactly as it did before the assault began. Without a moment's hesitation, the general returned to the lead truck, waived all his support personnel into the remaining army trucks that brought them and ordered his forces to remove themselves from the immediate area. After gaining a distance of 5 miles, the General halted his convoy. Then he picked up his intercom and quietly ordered the deployment of his MOAB Type II, Mother of All Bombs II, a new much more powerful version of the most powerful conventional weapon in the world. Within a half hour a C-130 transport lumbered overhead and dropped the massive conventional weapon on Edward's house. The concussive force of the detonated weapon rattled windows miles away and literally caused ground tremors. Satisfied with the deployment, General Porter returned to Edward's home to see the results.

The devastation outside of Edward's house had increased, the massive trees looked like burned matchsticks, but General Porter literally stood there dumbstruck when he observed no change in the shield itself. Obviously, no conventional weapon would affect this shield. He needed nuclear weapons. The General called his superiors and sought permission to deploy a nuclear artillery shell. What the General did not and could not know is that his actions to this point had already created a political nightmare for the President. Worse still, his various munitions had started at least four forest fires one of which burned out of control. The Governor of Montana, both of its Senators and single Congressman had already called for the President's resignation and/or impeachment. They said the President of the US had made war on their state.

General Porter without a Presidential authorization to obliterate the site with nuclear weapons ordered his personnel to begin digging. If he couldn't destroy the shield from the top, he would do so from the bottom. With a small backhoe, some portable digging machines and shovels, the General quickly dug a tunnel using one of the blast holes next to the main gate. At a depth of 8 feet, he first struck solid granite then the shield itself. Using several other blast holes including the trench in front of the gate, the General dug other tunnels but encountered the same rocky base and the shield from seven to eight feet in the ground. The General needed larger equipment that could penetrate the hard rock and go much deeper under the shield. He ordered his men back at the base in Wyoming to locate the tools and equipment he needed. General Porter would never give up until he had achieved his mission.

THE WHITE HOUSE

The President stared at his assembled cabinet and special invitees such as his Science Advisor, Terry Rothschild while he rubbed his temples. The raid on the scientist's home had not gone well. He spoke forcefully.

"I have to appear on national television and explain what happened on this ridiculous raid on the scientist's Montana property. Otherwise, I'm likely to be impeached by the Congress or thrown in jail by the courts. Conrad couldn't General Porter have waited for a search warrant? My actions might have been a little more defensible then."

"We did obtain a search warrant but General Porter didn't have it when he approached the homeowners. The General acted as he did because of the threat from North Korea, Russia and China. We have to be in a position to stop the Topol missile armed with the 50 megaton RDS 220 nuclear device. Edward's lasers are the best way to stop that missile. Only Edward can give us assurances that his lasers are properly adjusted and ready to fire. So far he has refused to speak with us let alone help us. We had no choice but to try to take him by force. We did what we felt to be necessary. As you will recall you ordered us to take him anyway we could."

"You went way overboard trampling the constitution in the process. To do that you detained my FBI agents who were supposed to run a joint operation with you. If I remember, only the FBI had jurisdiction in this matter. You obviously did not want us to remind you what was allowable and what was not. Now I have to lie through my teeth and declare that I had responsibility for this fiasco." FBI Director Tipton fumed.

"Tom, Secretary Conrad only did what I asked him to do. We face an imminent threat. We have to persuade the scientist to help us. When he refuses to speak with us, the scientist leaves us no choice. Still, I do not recall authorizing the use of our most powerful conventional bomb. That was overkill. It makes us look like thugs just as the scientist declared we are in his interview." The President said.

"Yes but why the military? We could have used another approach. Wait a minute. You wanted to test Edward's shield. That must be it." Tipton said.

"Yes this was part of it and I must say our entire military establishment is amazed. Edward produces technology that is so advanced we can barely comprehend it. As to the new type II MOAB, because the weapon is a conventional type, the General had authority to deploy it." Secretary Conrad said.

"If you wanted to destroy Edward's shields you should have used Edward's lasers." Chen the CIA Director said.

"We considered that but if we deployed his weapons he would merely have deactivated them. He might never activate them again. We are already on bad paper with him. After turning the area around his house into a wasteland and trying to kill him in the process, he may be even less willing to talk with us than he is now." Conrad said.

"I suppose the best thing to do is to put him and his girlfriend on the most FBI wanted list and have it posted on line and across the country in government buildings at all levels. We will have to invent a crime he has committed. So far, we seem to be the only ones violating the law. Although if we keep treating Edward this way, what will prevent him from simply emigrating to another country and taking his science with him? I don't even know why he is still in this country. We certainly have not made him feel welcome in his own country." Director Tipton said.

"I don't think he trusts the motives of any other government. At least in the US, he is a native and knows that legal rights matter although he may begin to doubt that after our strike on his Montana property. This is why it is important that there is some accountability for what happened there. I still have ways of talking to Edward or at least getting a message to him. I'm not sure after the strike he will be listening but we have to stop being so aggressive with Isaac. We have wasted a lot of time and resources with little to show for it except a presidential impeachment attempt on Capitol Hill." Science Advisor Rothschild said.

"Tom I suspected you had a way of reaching the scientist. Now Isaac will realize we mean business and will take political risks to gain access to his technology. Perhaps a soft approach can bring him to the table. You can tell Isaac that he will become the most wanted man in American if he chooses not to cooperate, but at the same time tell him we will guarantee his safety if he cooperates. The impeachment process just so you know is mostly for show. The leadership realizes the risks we face and will find a way not to advance the impeachment articles should it come to that." The President said.

"I'll work on it Mr. President but whatever you offer, Isaac will not want to give up his freedom. He doesn't want to be anyone's slave."

"He has no choice in the matter. The entire world wants what he has. There is simply no place on this planet for him to hide." The President replied.

"Mr. President, I can't approach Edward/Isaac with this attitude. He will never cooperate with us." Rothschild responded.

"Then lie to him. You do whatever it takes to gain Isaac's cooperation. Am I clear?" The President almost yelled.

"Yes sir." They all responded.

As the President's closest advisors left the President's office, the President motioned Conrad to stay. He approached the defense secretary with a very serious look on his face.

"Conrad, you must continue to use all options with Edward. If you cannot capture him kill him. Because we have his technology now, we have an advantage. If he goes to another country we will lose that advantage or maybe even surrender it."

"Yes Mr. President. This is what we are doing and will continue to do. I completely agree with your position on this matter." Conrad said.

THE OTHER SIDE OF THE STORY

As Edward and Mary Ann drove to Spokane, Edward arranged an on camera interview with a national television station. He set up the interview through a mounted laptop in the car. He turned to Mary Ann as he prepared to go on the air.

"Mary, I wanted to do this interview in the car for a variety of reasons. First, I wanted to subtly send the message that we weren't in the Montana house. This removes one of the army's reasons for invading our house. 2. Being mobile, helps me mask the signal so that our location is harder to pinpoint. Just don't jostle the car while I am talking. I don't want to look drunk." Edward smiled.

"Okay movie star I will keep the car straight." Mary Ann laughed.

A man's voice came over the speaker in the car.

"Edward are you there. This is Sam Holmes WWBC News. I'm ready to go live."

"Yes. Go ahead."

"Okay here we go. This is Sam Holmes WWBC news. I have an exclusive interview with Edward, the world's greatest scientist. He has invented a portal to allow people and material to go back and forth between Mars, our Moon, and Ganymede, Jupiter's and the Solar System's largest moon instantly as well as some other moons. He has also developed energy shields and advanced lasers that no one on Earth can match. He has literally created technology out of star wars. Today the US military and from some unconfirmed reports we have received, Russia and China, have attacked Edward's home in Northwest Montana near Glacier National Park, but have been unable to breach Edward's energy shields. I understand you are not in the house. Edward did you escape from there?"

"No I left there several days ago, but I observed the entire attack from cameras I installed inside the shield. I have already e-mailed these videos to all major news outlets, placed them on my web page sciedward.com and circulated them on the Internet."

"So what is your reaction to this army attack on your house?"

"An army general approached my house and demanded to search it. He had no search warrant. I refused this illegal entry as is my right. He reacted by declaring war on me. The general bombarded my house with an unprecedented number of bombs and missiles. The general concluded his assault with the deployment of a MOAB II, the largest conventional bomb made. My private property, beautiful woods and vistas, has been laid waste. From what I understand the bombardment triggered several damaging forest fires. I'm a private citizen with rights guaranteed by the constitution. The general violated those rights in a way that would have made a Nazi SS Commander proud. He is nothing more than a thug without any respect for our laws. On top of all this, my understanding is that the military is not allowed to undertake such missions against Americans on American soil. Apparently this general has not read the memo. My attorneys will be addressing these issues in court. This is of course why I have refused to provide any more weapons or shields to our military or to adjust and maintain the weapons I have already provided them. People like the general shouldn't even be allowed to have a gun permit. He cannot be trusted to make rational decisions."

"But General Porter did have some justification for his actions. We have unconfirmed reports that the North Koreans intend to launch an advanced soviet ICBM equipped with Russia's most powerful nuclear weapon at Yellowstone National Park. If the Yellowstone Super Volcano were to erupt as a result, the ash alone would cover the US killing people, plants and animals and leaving us a ruined nation. Your weapon systems are the best protection against such an attack."

"Then, if these reports are true, I will adjust the shields and lasers so they can be effective but I will not give the military any more weapons. Also, I will not give up my freedom to become a slave to the US Government. I only want to make defensive weapons and portals to allows us to explore and colonize the solar system." Edward responded.

"Why don't you turn yourself in to the authorities?"

"First I haven't done anything wrong. I am the victim of government aggression. Also, you seem to have forgotten what just happened. The US Army tried to murder us. Why would I turn myself into them? Would you?" Edward said.

"You make a good point. What will you do now? The government will find you."

"Do what I always do. Invent things beyond the world's understanding or comprehension. Now I need to end this conversation. I'm getting to a point where my various tricks to prevent the authorities from pinpointing my interview location will fail. Goodbye."

After Edward terminated the connection, Mary Ann spoke.

"Edward you didn't mention me or our music. Why?"

"I wanted to protect you and our ability to make music. The more they know about us the greater danger we face."

"Do you think our disguises will hide us?"

"They have so far. You look pretty good as a disheveled singer and artist. I just look weird which I guess is a good thing."

"I can't wait to arrive in Spokane and begin our performances."

"Me too. I don't know how much time we have, but I intend to enjoy every moment." Edward said with a smile.

SPOKANE

Edward and Mary Ann checked into the Days Inn as Bill and Dorothy Davis. No one seemed to recognize them in their outfits. The government had of course circulated their pictures widely. The use of colored contact lenses changing Mary Ann eyes from violet to blue and Edward's brown eyes to blue helped most of all.

After unpacking their suitcases, they drove to a music store where they saw advertised the sale of an older fender guitar. Edward left his collection of guitars at his Montana home. He had not wanted to use a guitar that his pursuers might identify with him. The bright red fender with sparkles this store offered did not resemble any guitar he presently owned. After carefully examining the guitar, Edward purchased the instrument along with a good amplifier and some picks. Then both of them drove to the Lazy Daisy Susan, the bar/nightclub where they would perform. As they left the car to enter the nightclub Edward remarked.

"We have to focus on our performances and try to avoid conflict of any kind. We cannot afford to draw any unwanted attention. With a beautiful woman like you violet eyes or not, guys filled with alcohol can and will provide problems. The personal shield I placed under the skin of each of our backs will provide us safety but at the same time if we have to use them our gig here will be done. The authorities will be upon us before we know it."

"Edward I know, but we can't think about all that. We have to just perform and enjoy ourselves."

"Then let's go and do just that."

"The bar met both of their expectations. They ate a little food and patiently waited while karaoke and other acts preceded them. Finally at around 8 pm, Edward and Mary Ann took the stage. Gus the owner treated them well and they felt very comfortable when they took the stage. Edward began the set with a blistering guitar run, which led into a couple of Stevie Ray Vaughn tunes. They followed with a variety of blues, pop and country songs. The audience seem appreciative and the more they played the happier Edward and Mary Ann seemed. They found their element and thoroughly enjoyed it. When their time ended at 10 pm, the crowd wanted more but Gus ended their program saying simply.

"We don't do encores at the Lazy Daisy Susan, but thanks for coming out. Bill and Dorothy will be performing every night this week. If you want to hear more of them, come back tomorrow night. Now we have our final act of he night--the Impressionaires.

Happy with their performances, Edward and Mary Ann shook Gus' hand and prepared to leave. Gus said.

"Both of you are really terrific. I think when the word gets around our crowds will grow. Edward you have to be the best electric guitarist I have ever heard even better than the great Billy Ray Vaughn. I think I recognize the guitar. A guy named Silas owned it. He played here but was not in your league. He had a gambling problem, which is why I guess you ended up with his guitar. You can hang around the bar a little longer if you want or otherwise I will see you tomorrow night. Here is your fee for the night. You earned it."

"Thanks Gus. Yeah we are a little tired. We drove a long way today to get here. We will see you tomorrow night." As Mary Ann and Edward began to leave, both of them noticed a huge guy in the corner. He followed Mary Ann with his eyes.

Later that night in the hotel room, Mary Ann said.

"That huge guy at the bar creeped me out. He seemed hungry and I appeared as the only item on the menu. He can't touch me can he?"

"No, the shield protects you completely. Still I know what you mean. The guy is trouble. Let's ask Gus what he knows about the guy."

"Good idea. Besides him I had a great time."

"So did I Mary Ann. So did I."

The next day, Mary Ann and Edward toured Spokane in their disguises. They liked the medium size city and the people they met. They didn't arrive at the Lazy Daisy Susan until 7 pm following a nice leisurely meal. To their astonishment, the crowd doubled in size. The big man sat where he had the previous night. Edward and Mary Ann sat with Gus. Edward immediately launched into a conversation.

"Gus that big guy over there is making us a little nervous. What is with him?"

"Seth you mean. The man has quite a story. Ten years ago, Seth right out of high school became an auto mechanic. Seth had average intelligence and a quiet nice way about him. He came in here from time to time when he came of age. Right after becoming a mechanic, Seth started bodybuilding. Reportedly, he took heavy doses of steroids and vitamins to help him grow. The more drugs he took the harder he worked out. Within a year he had almost doubled in size. Seth just kept on growing as if something possessed him. His personality also changed. He became aggressive and somewhat nasty. Last year, his bodybuilding paid off when he won runner up at the Mr. Washington State contest. Seth almost won. This year he is expected to win as last year's winner became ill. Seth quit his job as a mechanic and spends his time doing ads and promotions for various vitamin and body building products. He lives in an apartment not far from here. I banned him from the bar 6 months ago because of an incident with one of my pretty waitresses. He pursued here aggressively but she repeatedly told him no. She told me Seth scared her. One night he just grabbed the poor girl and started to haul her away. I called the police and had him arrested. He received probation. The girl quit and moved away. The incident has faded over time. Seth returned to the bar after 6 months and hasn't provided any problems since. Still, I worry about him. Those steroids do weird things to you. I noticed he had his eyes on you Mary Ann. I told him to cool it after you left last night. He said he would."

"Gus obviously we want nothing to do with Seth. If he comes after Mary Ann, there will be trouble." Edward said.

"Yeah I know. I think I have it covered. The next time Seth gets in trouble the judge told him that he would spend time behind bars. Seth has his big meet coming up in a few days. He won't do anything to jeopardize what he believes to be his big chance."

"I hope you're right." Edward said.

The next several days went well. Edward and Mary Ann performed each night to increasingly larger crowds. They toured the area around the city during the day and sometimes the nearby mountains and performed at night. Spokane fit them well. Edward to lessen the heat on both of them fixed the maintenance issues on both the militaries shields and lasers and let the pentagon know he had done so. As a result the high profile attacks on them seem to lessen. Yet both Edward and Mary Ann knew that the pursuit continued, albeit at a reduced level.

Seth, however, continued to be a problem. Every night he sat at the same seat and spent their entire performance staring at Mary Ann. No one dared challenge him. Some fourteen additional days passed this way. Toward the end of this time, Seth disappeared for three days. Finally, on the seventeenth night everything changed. Seth returned and he looked and acted differently. The Spokane papers carried his story. As expected, he became Mr. Washington State and according to the paper would be one of the top contenders in the Mr. America pageant scheduled in another month.

After the end of their final set, a tired Edward and Mary Ann quickly exited the bar and headed for their car. Unlike most nights, they spent very little time with their many fans. The couple just wanted some sleep. When they reached their car, Seth suddenly stepped in front of them, showing off his huge biceps. He spoke in a confident and aggressive way.

"You know who I am? You must have seen me watching you."

"Yes, we noticed you Seth. You are one of our most devoted fans, but tonight my wife Mary Ann and I just want to go home and get some sleep. Performing this way every evening can be exhausting."

Turning to Mary Ann (Dorothy), Seth spoke again.

"Your husband is a scrawny loser. I'm Mr. Washington State and may soon become Mr. America. You need to be with me."

"No I don't. I'm with my husband who is the finest guitar player in the world. I'm not into muscle guys. If I'm not mistaken according to Gus, one more assault on a woman puts you in jail. You are getting pretty close to that right now." Mary Ann said angrily.

Seth went to grab Mary Ann and Edward quickly stepped in his way. The big man drew back his massive fist and snarled.

"Either you move or I will flatten you like a pancake."

"I'm not going anywhere. You will regret coming after me. I can assure you of that."

With all his strength, Seth swung at Edward's chin. Edward's shield activated and Seth's hand hit the shield with incredible force. The bones in Seth's hand shattered with a very loud crack. The big men fell to the ground in pain. As

Seth moaned clutching his ruined hand, Edward said calmly.

"Seth you really should be more careful with how you swing your fist. Even a muscle man like you can't beat up a car."

Edward and Mary Ann left quickly before Seth could respond. The next day, Edward bought an extra large glove and filled it with rocks. Then he used it to hit the side of their car that faced the sidewalk last night as hard as he could. With the dent in place, Edward tried to scrape a little of the DNA Seth left on Edward's shield when Seth hit it. Edward rubbed what he managed to scrape on the car dent. While Edward and Mary Ann had no intention of filing a police report on the incident, they wanted to be prepared with a plausible story if the matter became public. That evening Gus took Mary Ann and Edward aside when they entered the bar.

"Seth had three hours of surgery on his hand last night. I saw him go after you with a determined look on his face. I even followed him a ways. He won't tell anyone what happened."

"Seth confronted me last night and demanded that I be with him. Edward intervened. Seth took a swing at Edward but Edward ducked and Seth hit the side of our car instead. We can show you the dent. Seth may be a great body builder but he is a lousy boxer." Mary Ann said.

"I thought it might be something like that. Seth is in a bad way. He won't be able to compete now in the Mr. America contest. He blames you for his troubles. There is no telling what he will do. You will have to be careful around him."

"We will be. We have no plans to file any charges against Seth. We just want to be left alone."

"Let's hope Seth feels the same way."

As Edward and Mary Ann left the bar that evening a pretty young reporter approached them.

"HI I'm Kim with the Spokane Reporter. My sources inform me that Seth our body builder champion obtained his injuries fighting you."

"Seth aggressively came after me when we reached our car. Edward stepped in front of me. Seth threw a punch at Edward but Edward ducked just in time. Seth's fist hit our car instead putting a big dent in it. That's pretty much the story. Neither of us had met Seth prior to that point. I guess the guy has a habit of fixating on girls. I happen to be his latest target." Mary Ann said.

"Yeah that makes sense. Seth, as you say, has a history of going after women. I know this doesn't make any sense but Seth claims he hit your chin and that was what broke his hand."

"Well you can see my chin. Does it look like a body builder hit it with his fist? Come on we will show you the dent in the car." Edward said.

"Yeah sure. As a reporter, I couldn't really give Seth's story any credence. The dent in the car would explain everything."

After Edward showed Kim the dent, she took a picture of it and smiling turned to the couple.

"Looks like a big fist hit the car. Maybe Seth had been drinking and didn't realize what he hit."

"Yeah, Seth goes through several drinks a night at the same table. He almost never misses our shows. We always thought he would introduce himself as other fans have but until last night we never talked to him. He must have had more drinks than usual last night." Mary Ann said.

"Okay. I think that finishes my story except for one thing. Did you file a complaint against Seth? I haven't heard of one."

"No. We decided not to file a complaint. Seth didn't have the opportunity to lay his hands on Mary Ann and of course he is the only one who suffered any injuries. When you are entertainers like us, some fans become obsessed, particularly with a beautiful woman like my wife. Still, if he comes after us again, we will file.' Edward said.

'Alright; here is my card. If you think of anything else, call me." Kim said as she walked away into the night.

When Edward and Mary Ann returned to their hotel room, they both sat at the small table in their room. Edward said with some certainty.

"Mary Ann unfortunately, we will have to leave. If our pursuers read the story Kim will write, they may very well decide to come here and investigate us. The weak part of our story is Seth hitting the car door with his fist. Seth played high school football. He is not uncoordinated. He wouldn't punch a car door. As both of us know, I didn't stand in front of the car. If carefully investigated the story could fall apart. An investigator, like our pursuers will see all this. The people pursuing us know of my shields. We will have a particularly hard time escaping attention if the paper prints Seth's version of the encounter. What sounds like nonsense to most people will make sense to our pursuers." Edward said.

"You're right of course. We'll tell Gus tonight and leave tomorrow. I'm sorry this had to end. I really liked our crowds."

"So did I but the government has not shown itself to be very friendly to us."

"Where will we go?"

"We have two choices. We can return to the Montana house or go to my alternate house in Anchorage. They won't be expecting us to return to the Glacier National Park home. Also, after the attack, my shield turned opaque. You can't see anything going on inside. So, we can operate there in relative safety. Of course, they know nothing about the

Anchorage home. This house, which is almost as large as the Montana house, would provide a nice refuge. What do you think?"

"If we can return safely to the Montana house, let's go there."

"Then we will." Edward said but with a little hesitation. The Anchorage home would be safer but if Mary Ann wanted to return to Montana he would oblige her. This whole ordeal had to have been tough on her. He could make this change in their plans.

THE TRIP BACK

Susan packed or sold most of her things. She intended to leave the US and never return. She had found a job as an interpreter in Bolivia. Susan spoke five languages; ironically Mandarin being her poorest, and this country had recently removed its reciprocity arrangement with the US. She could disappear there with relative ease. Susan had an emotional and dramatic last meeting with her parents last night, accusing her father of forcing her into being a spy. Now she had to leave the US or be arrested and tried as a traitor. She told him that she never wanted to speak or hear from him again.

Before she could get out the door to make her flight to Toronto from where she would make her way to Bolivia, her cell phone rang. She recognized the number and reluctantly answered the phone.

"Yes."

"Susan you can't just run away. You are a spy and you will remain a spy until we say otherwise. If you had taken that flight to Toronto, you would have been tagged as a possible terrorist and detained. If you had managed to make your flight to Bolivia, you would have been denied entry. If and when the US targets you, we will provide a means for you to escape. In the meantime, we have work for you to do. As you know, Edward and Mary Ann remain at large. China, Russia, and the US all failed to kidnap the couple or gain access to Edward's inventions. We want you to find them again unless of course you want to become the target of an FBI investigation of espionage."

"I should have known that escape would become impossible for me. I will of course, do as you ask but don't ever use my father as leverage on me again. As far as I am concerned, the greedy self centered traitor can rot in hell."

"Duly noted but of course this changes nothing. I will send you some information we have that may help you in your search. Good luck and I will be in touch."

A visibly angry Susan sat at her computer in her near empty room. She would soon restore the furniture and decorations that hadn't been sold to the place. Fortunately, although she had some low offers, Susan had not yet agreed on a sale price for her condo. She would now withdraw her condo from the market. Susan subscribed to a clipping service she used to track down unusual local news stories. Susan decided to limit the search to the North Western US but of course had no assurances that Edward and Mary Ann remained in this area. After reading local articles for three hours in this area, sitting in her solitary room, one finally caught her eye.

Mr. Washington State breaks hand in pursuit of Married Woman

Seth Paduch, Mr. Washington State and a local resident, according to several witnesses including the intended victims, aggressively pursued Dorothy Davis part of the popular Bill and Dorothy Davis singing team that has drawn record crowds at the Lazy Daisy Susan Bar. Bill confronted Seth when he threatened his wife Dorothy. Seth took a swing at his rival but the body builder missed Bill and crashed his fist into Bill's car, badly fracturing his hand. Seth claims that he hit Bill's chin with his fist but since Bill shows no signs of being hit that seems unlikely. This is not the first problem our bodybuilding champion has had. Seth received a probationary sentence for attacking a waitress at the same bar several years ago. Seth, an early favorite to win the Mr. America contest next month will now have to skip the competition. His hand will not heal in time to compete.

Accustomed to acting on her hunches, Susan headed to the airport to take a flight to Spokane not Toronto as she first planned. As Susan recalled from her earlier pursuit, Mary Ann sung and Edward/Isaac as a musical genius could play any instrument. Also, Seth could have crashed his fist into one of Edward's shields.

At the same time Susan boarded a flight so did Rich and Rose. They hadn't seen the article but an alert citizen said that a couple matching Edward and Mary Ann's description obtained some gas at her station outside Spokane. According to this woman, they wore convincing disguises but she had earlier in her career worked for the Spokane PD in the missing persons division and had developed some skill in seeing through disguises.

Rich turned to Rose as they boarded their flight to Spokane.

"Rose what would Edward and Mary Ann be doing in Spokane of all places other than it is fairly close to Glacier National Park? What is the attraction? "

"I don't know. They both like music at least according to our best intelligence but Spokane isn't necessarily a hot spot for music."

"Yeah it could be something like this. Edward will want to do things with Mary Ann. No one on Earth can share his science interests very well. So something like this makes sense."

"Okay while we fly I'm going to find everything I can on the music scene in Spokane. There might be a clue. After several hours of Internet work, Rose finally encountered the newspaper story that interested Susan. She exclaimed.

"This is it. They are working at the Lazy Daisy Susan. A body builder went after May Ann and tried to punch Edward to get to her. He ended up with a fractured hand. My guess is he encountered one of Edward's energy shields. He must have developed a small one for individuals. Apparently, Edward and Mary Ann's show is very popular."

"Sounds right but we had better hurry once we get to Spokane. My guess is they are headed out of town after that article appeared."

"Yeah if they have any sense they would be." Mary Ann responded.

"We should report this lead to our FBI handlers. We owe them a report with some useful information. Otherwise, we could lose our contract." Rich added.

Early in the morning, Edward and Mary Ann drove back toward Montana the same way they had come into Spokane. They had filled the SUV with gas before they left. Gus tried to persuade them to stay, but Mary Ann and Edward told him that the situation with Seth had become a problem they no longer wanted to face. They had very little sleep before their departure. Edward drove while Mary Ann slept.

One hour into their journey, Mary Ann woke and they began to have a conversation. Mary Ann spoke first.

"How much longer can we do this: moving from place to place? Our government, heck all of the world's major governments will keep coming after us."

"Honestly I don't know. I thought we could be clever enough to hide for a while but so far this hasn't been the case. I have already served as a virtual prisoner of the government. I don't want to repeat that experience. At the back of my mind, I have had an alternate plan.

"The US government has always maintained an undisclosed ancient site, which has technology that looks like what I created to transport people to our nearby planets, at their Air Force base near Anchorage. Being inside the government, I finally found some information on it. At least at that point, they could not enter the site or understand its purpose and design. I'm convinced it is an interstellar portal for organic and inorganic material similar to what I developed. I have long felt as have other people studying me that I have a genetic memory for the technology developed by this ancient and very advanced race. If so, I may be able to enter this facility and utilize it. When I asked my superiors for the opportunity to do this, they turned me down. They said I could be put in jail for merely bringing up the subject. I think this started the bad relations between me and my bosses and the military who eventually took over my project. They wanted me to shut up and take orders, which I never wanted to do.

"If I am right about what this site really is, I can use it to transport myself to the world of the ancients and gain a fuller understanding of my genetic memory and science talents. After I have this knowledge, I can return to Earth and know what I am sharing with the public and the science community. Obviously, there are great personal risks for me from those who want to kill or capture me as well as those risks associated with trying to use an ancient technology that might not work any more.

I would be more than willing to assume those risks if it were not for you. I want to spend my time with you, not take off across the galaxy.

"So in answer to your question, we can keep doing this as long as you want to do so. When it becomes unbearable, and you want to put a stop to it all, then I can try to leave Earth. "

"For now, let's keep to the plan: return to Montana and live at the home where they do not think we are living. If the pursuit becomes too great, we can consider your plan. I'm not sure I want to head to Alaska right now."

"Okay we will stick to the plan Mary Ann."

At just this moment, they heard a loud low flying jet coming from behind them. Edward turned to look at the jet, a Warthog, with two large missiles attached to it. Edward remarked.

"This is strange. The aircraft looks like it is attacking us. Those are Hellfire Missiles on the Warthog's wings. My god, one of the missiles is detaching and heading for us. I can see it out of my rearview mirror. I'll stop the car. Maybe the missile will overfly us. I'm locking my cameras on this and making sure it is uploaded to the Internet at least as long as the camera continues to work." Edward said.

Earlier, Rose and Rich then Susan drove to the Lazy Daisy Susan looking for Gus. Rich and Rose for once made it there first. Gus, who had just arrived at his bar greeted the two warmly and seemed impressed by their credentials.

"So the FBI is it. What can I do to help you?" Gus said.

"We are curious about the husband and wife team who performed at your bar. What can you tell me about them?"

"Bill and Dorothy Davis are the most talented people I ever had perform at my bar. Bill may be the best electric guitar artist who has ever lived. Dorothy had a nice pleasant singing voice to add some dimension to Bill and is one of the most beautiful women I have ever met. Every time they performed, my place reached capacity and beyond. I don't know why they left. Perhaps, Seth, Mr. Washington State had something to do with it. He really lusted after Mary Ann. That is about all I know." Gus said.

"Do you have any idea where they went or what kind of car they drove? It is important. We need to find these individuals as soon as possible." Rose said.

"They mentioned Montana but they obviously are not native to the state. Perhaps they went there on Interstate 90. I don't know. As to their car, the night of the incident with Seth, I followed Seth out of the bar to see if he went after Bill and Dorothy. I saw Seth collapse to the ground when he hit the car with his fist but I didn't see him throw the punch. The car he hit was a new Navy Blue Chevrolet Tahoe, but I don't remember the license plate. It will of course be easy to spot with a dent in the driver's side. Bill and Dorothy took off after checking to see if Seth could walk. He hurled insults at them but did not attack them again. That is all I know. I called an ambulance for Seth and stayed with him until it came. He wouldn't talk to me about the incident except to say that if he told me what happened I wouldn't believe him."

"That is helpful. Can you think about anything else unusual about the couple?"

"They were very nice. Both of them wore contacts, the same bright blue, which led me to believe they didn't need glasses. Edward I think wore a wig and beard. They both dressed in casual almost scruffy clothes. To be frank, they seemed to be wearing disguises. I never asked them about it. I just wanted them to perform. Are they in some kind of trouble?" Gus said.

"No not really. The government just wants to talk with Edward. By the way, if a beautiful Chinese girl comes here asking questions she is a Chinese spy. Don't give her any information. We are watching her very carefully. Thanks for all your help." Rich said.

Rich passed on the information they had learned from Gus to his contacts in the FBI. He asked them if they wanted Rose and him to follow the couple by car assuming they went back toward Montana. Their contact said no. They had done their job. They could return to Chicago. After the phone call, Rich turned to Rose with concern on his face.

"I find it a little strange that our FBI contact didn't want us to follow Edward and Mary Ann. I didn't like the way the military reacted to us finding Edward last time. They launched an all out war like assault on his private home we found. I have a feeling that they will use military resources to go after them again. It is creepy and very un American." Rich said.

"Yeah I feel the same way. Maybe we should forget this gig. Let them pay us until they ask for us to do more tracking if they do. Then we can excuse ourselves."

"Yeah let's do that. The money is great but this whole thing runs against my grain." Rich said.

After the missile release, Edward and Mary Ann's world slowed down. Edward brought the car to a stop. Their shield's activated and then the missile descended on their vehicle. The explosion that occurred seconds later created a brilliant world like the center of the sun but strangely neither Edward nor Mary Ann could feel any heat. They closed their eyes the moment the flash began to protect their eyes. Then they could feel themselves hurling through the space of the torn remnants of their SUV. Both of them hit the pavement and rolled off the road into a ditch. As they hurled through the air, several pieces of the car struck the outside of their shields but deflected off in another direction. Their shields kept their bodies in a rigid frozen position. None of the powerful forces around them twisted or impacted their bodies. After several minutes, Edward and Mary Ann struggled to their feet. Edward spoke immediately.

"Mary Ann, are you hurt? I don't think I am. I had no idea these personal shields could withstand this kind of punishment."

"No other than shaking a little from the fear I'm fine. One of the strangest parts of that experience is that I heard no sound, none at all. The force of that blast should have blown apart our ear drums."

"Yes. The shields protected us from every possible hazard. Even I'm not sure how they did that. We need to get moving. There is another road that intersects this one on an angle about a mile to the North. If we head into the woods we should intersect it. The police will be here soon. They will have to close this road. There is a huge crater in the middle of it. Also, the military will come down here to investigate. If people talk with us, we will have to maintain that we know nothing about this incident. We just heard it in the distance."

"Yes that makes sense. I would like to curl up in a ball after that experience but we need to concentrate on surviving. Let's go."

After some difficult hiking and the siting of a grizzly bear in the distance, Edward and Mary Ann walked onto a smaller state road. According to some information Edward found on his phone, which was undamaged inside his shield, a small restaurant and gas station lay about a mile down this road where it intersected with Interstate 90. Edward and Mary Ann walked at a normal pace toward the facility. In twenty minutes they reached the restaurant with its log cabin exterior and country feel. They ordered some coffee and two hamburgers. They started to carefully plan their next moves. Edward spoke first after excusing himself to use the phone.

"I located a used car dealership in the next town and purchased a used Ford Explorer with only 25,000 miles. The dealer is delivering the car here in about a half hour. I have already taken care of the registration. As to our former car, I dare not file an insurance claim. How do I explain a Hell Fire missile hit it? I propose we head toward Montana but take the next exit and work our way back toward Interstate 90 West beyond the place the missile hit took place. We will then drive to Anchorage and to my other house. This is a long journey but I don't know where else to go. They will be after us once they realize there are no bodies or rather body parts anywhere near the bomb site. The first place they will go is Montana, assuming we were headed there."

"Yeah, I wanted to spend some time in Montana but I guess it doesn't make any sense after all. What is the Anchorage house like?"

"Very nice and self contained. I think you will like it. Now we have to find a way to get there. Maybe a ferry is the best idea. I don't want to cross into Canada and back out again. Both Canadian and US official will be looking for us."

PURSUIT

Susan then Rich and Rose found nothing in Montana. The army had switched to a strategy of undermining the house by attacking the entire stone structure upon which the house rested. The local federal court issued a mandamus and injunction against the army in an attempt to stop their efforts but the army merely ignored the court orders. The court responded by issuing arrest warrants for General Porter and his staff but neither local law enforcement or the FBI seemed capable of enforcing the orders. The work continued with armed soldiers guarding the work site. The President's disregard for the orders of the federal court worsened the constitutional crisis in Washington. The Montana congressman's impeachment resolution gained new steam and had already been reported to the floor. The media wanted the President arrested.

The President's case had also been seriously undermined when he had to admit that Edward fixed the energy shields and lasers he supplied the military. Even though the fix appeared to be a temporary one, the US now had fully functional super weapons at their disposal. When North Korea made another foolish threat, the US used the weapons to totally disarm the North Koreans, wiping out every missile, nuclear device, plane, artillery piece, and military facility in the country. Their large army had little more than hand weapons left with which to fight anyone and even those had been depleted. The threat to the US evaporated.

The Hellfire missile attack, however, changed the situation. Edward responded to the attack by disabling his shields and lasers used by the military. A new effort began to supply North Korea once again with the same missiles and nuclear bombs the US destroyed. North Korea in total chaos after the disarming of their military vowed to use the missiles but no longer had a place to launch them. Also, a North Korean civil war began after the public became aware that the military lost most of its strength. The US once again threatened nuclear war if North Korea deployed the new missile.

General Porter ignored all of it. He just kept digging. When Rich and Rose spoke with him identifying themselves as the ones who found Edward and Mary Ann, the General merely stated that he had his orders and would continue to carry them out until told otherwise. A frustrated Rich and Rose, after returning to their hotel, discussed what to do next.

"Where could they have gone? We need a lead. We have no good pictures of them in their disguises. An FBI agent in Spokane did find a fan of theirs who took a poor quality picture of them on stage but this doesn't help very much. Our photography experts are trying to enhance the picture and get it out on the wires but we are probably a day away from them doing that. For all we know they have changed their disguises

"Let's reconstruct everything we know. They clearly left the city and if the air force is correct their car was sighted going toward Montana. The air force picture even shows the dent in the passenger side. This is why they took the car out with a Hellfire missile which pardon me for saying was a very dumb ****ing move. Apparently, Edward's and Mary Ann's shields as impossible as it seems prevented them from sustaining any injuries. They then left the site and according to some reports a husband and wife couple, who may or may not be Edward and Mary Ann bought a car from a nearby town and headed toward Montana. At this point, we have no more information or reports. The car they purchased a used but fairly new Black Ford Explorer has not been spotted since they drove away with it. We must assume Edward changed the color of the vehicle and put new plates on it. We still, however, have no clue where they went or why."

"Yeah that sums it all up. We need to get in Mary Ann and Edward's heads. Clearly they are angry about the Hellfire attack. Why wouldn't they be? What I don't see is where they can go or what they can do. They are out of options. Wait a minute. In one of our briefing books, the Department of Energy mentioned Isaac's interest in an alleged ancient site in Alaska near the Eielson Air Force Base. Apparently, Isaac believed it to be from the same race that he thinks is responsible for many of the very advanced devices he designs. From the time he learned of this site, he has expressed a desire to see the site but the military has blocked him from doing so. Perhaps, he went to Alaska. I don't know but it's certainly possible."

"Rich you have good memory, I don't remember that at all but it would make sense. Edward needs to find out who he is and why he can develop these very advanced technical marvels. If he indeed wants to go to this site, how will he do so? The military is all over him and have tried to kill him at least twice." Rose said.

"I don't know but we need to go to Anchorage and see what we can find." Rich responded.

"Wait a minute I thought we were going to quit this pursuit." Rose said.

"I think we will be better off resigning after Anchorage. I don't want to get on the bad side of the military on this one. The constitution doesn't allow them to do what they are doing but they are doing it anyway. I don't want to be on their bad side. Anyway, whoever they hire to replace us will probably be less sympathetic to Edward and Mary Ann than we are. We are actually doing them a favor by staying on the job."

"Okay this shouldn't take long but we need to bow out after this." Rose said.

"We will." Rich answered.

ALASKA

Edward and Mary Ann boarded a private jet chartered by Edward at Boeing field in Seattle. They retained their colored contacts, changed their hair color and wore very plain clothes. They also changed their faces in subtle ways with makeup. Edward continued to work on their appearance until facial recognition software no longer recognized either one of them. They traveled as Tom and Cynthia Thomas, civil engineers from Elmhurst, Illinois. They decided not to board a ferry. They felt too exposed being on a boat for such a long time. Surprisingly their disguises worked well. They flew without incident to Anchorage. Within 30 minutes of landing, they had rented a car and taken off for Edward's second home, purchased on the Internet. The home lay near the Eielson Air force base Edward wanted to visit.

The home, which had a nice view of the mountains, closely resembled their Montana home in size and layout. Many animals roamed outside of their shield including some very large Grisly Bears. Mary Ann worked on a novel while Edward worked on one of his many science projects. Edward also spent a great deal of time researching information on the ancient site at Eielson. He found a local who had made the investigation of this site his life's work. Edward found Mary Ann in her study and mentioned the man.

"A man named Jeffrey has investigated the ancient site. As an air force veteran, he guarded the ancient area for many years and became intrigued with it. Jeffrey wrote some articles on the site but the air force managed to discredit them. He lives near us. We should pay him a visit.

Jeffrey may have some information that will prove crucial to my attempt to access the site."

"Edward I don't know what I can add but a visit outside this house might be a nice diversion. I'll go along."

Fifty minutes later thanks to GPS tracking on their cell phones, they parked in front of Jeffrey's modest house. A dog barked but he didn't sound too menacing. After knocking the door, they moved back as the door opened. A late middle age man stared at both of them; then a smile crossed his face.

"Isaac, I knew you would come. This must be your wife Mary Ann as beautiful as the papers said she would be. We have much to discuss. Come in."

To Edward and Mary Ann's surprise, pictures of the ancient site lined the walls. Jeffrey even had a picture of the impenetrable door that led to the interior of the site. On the table, books and magazines about the ancient site lay open. Jeffrey once again spoke.

"Have a seat. I have a story to tell you Isaac. Thirty years ago, as a young airman, I guarded your father's lab at Eielson. Actually, I had some technical training, so I helped with some of the experiments as well. Your father the lead scientist at the lab found a very unusual rock near the site. Your mother the senior technician worked closely with your father on the rock. One day, your mother and father exposed the rock to increasing amounts of heat. At around one thousand degrees, the rock opened and a mist came forth. Both your father and mother, very near to the rock, breathed in large quantities of the mist. The rest of us in the lab breathed in less of it. When the mist disappeared, the rock became relatively inert. Despite many hours of effort, no more could be learned from it. Eventually, after exposure to the mist, your mother and father became romantically involved and married after she became pregnant with you. While your mother and father reported feeling strange and weird after ingesting the mist, their health remained good. After many years at the site, your father and mother moved to another research facility when no more could be learned from this site. Despite what now amounts to almost 40 years of effort, the air force never gained access to the interior of the site. The door on the side close to the base and the door on the opposite side in the forest could not be opened. Bombs, acid, drills, excavating machines, and other tools and explosives had no effect on the door or the cylinder that makes up the site. As best we could tell, a shield prevented us from even accessing the metal that made up the cylinder.

'All of us exposed to the mist including you mother and father began to have bizarre dreams involving another race of intelligent beings but the mist gave us no special powers or abilities to access the site. Believe me, we tried. After your parents left, I continued to correspond with them. They began to suspect that the principal effect of the gas appeared in you Isaac. Your brilliance confounded everyone that tested you. Your knowledge of science, physics, mathematics, engineering seemed almost otherworldly. Your parents, of course, died, your father long before your mother, but no evidence could be found linking the inhalation of the mist to their deaths. Rumors did persist however, that the military poisoned your father then your mother because of the secrets they held.

"We all feared what happened to them would happen to you. We know the military too well. What the military cannot control it kills. This is exactly what they are trying to do to you. Because of your very advanced technology, they have not been able to do so, but they won't stop trying. They stay up at night worrying that their enemies will somehow gain control of you and your technology. So you must enter the site and see what if anything the site can do to protect you. We have long theorized that the site contains a transportation device similar to the one you developed that can take you to the aliens' home world. There you can be safe. I don't know how to make you safe here. As to you Mary Ann, you may not have Isaac much longer."

"Jeffrey, I have long known that Edward's and my time together would be brief. I decided to take the ride anyway. We will do what we can to protect him. So can you take us to the ancient site? Do you have a way in?"

"In that regard, you're lucky. When the military finally realized they couldn't access the site, they diverted resources away from it. They only have a single guard on the base side entrance. They no longer have a guard on the forest entrance. They buried that entrance but I know where it is. If I'm right, your hand placed on the site's keypad will give us access to the site. When your father, mother and I realized that your hand might, the military had already removed their access to the site. I tried to convince my superiors that Isaac could give them access but they still denied the request. I never understood why. In any case, we shall soon discover if you have this power. Do you want to go to the site now? There is no reason to wait. We can take my car. It will be less recognizable than your own."

"Well what do you think Mary Ann? Should I seek my destiny right now or wait?" Edward said.

"You know the answer to that question as well as I do. Eventually, the military will figure out how to penetrate our shields. Then they will arrest or kill you and me as well. I will be collateral damage. Also, they will find us up here. We really don't have much of a choice. We have to go."

"Okay Jeffrey. Lead on. We will see if the universe awaits me. On the way over to the site, I will once again reset the shields and lasers for the US military. I may not have another opportunity to do so." Edward said.

THE AMERICANS AND THE CHINESE

For the first time in their long pursuit, Rose and Rich and Susan arrived with twenty minutes of each other at the Anchorage airport. Rose checked a suitcase so when she and Rich walked out of the terminal they bumped into Susan. They both stared at each other not knowing what to say. Finally, Rich spoke.

"Well if it isn't the Chinese spy Susan Wang. As usual we arrive at the same time and place. I've read your dossier, as well as those of many other spies from other countries. All our countries have made a terrible mess out of this Edward/Isaac affair, but our country has been the worst offender. Edward is after all a US citizen as is his wife Mary Ann but we have all treated them as the greatest threat to this world. They aren't. The threat is our countries using Edward's advanced science to threaten the rest of the world. Since we don't understand Edward or his science we send people to kill him. Our jobs are to put our countries in the position where they can carry out that threat. Although I have been paid well for this, the entire mission makes me feel dirty."

"Obviously, I can't admit I'm a spy for the Chinese government. As an American citizen this would make me a traitor and subject to a number of criminal laws. Nonetheless, like you I have been charged with the mission of finding Edward. I will do so but I have no personal desire to do so. Everything I do I do without a choice. If you want to cooperate this time, I am fine with that. Once I find Edward it is for others to decide what to do next." Susan said.

"Strangely enough this makes sense. We do our jobs and leave. Our countries can decide what to do next. So far what they have done is a disaster. I admire Edward. All he wants to do is to advance science but our governments are making this impossible for him to do." Rose said.

"Okay we are going to cooperate but what does this mean? We can't be seen together but maybe we can text back and forth with leads and ideas. Right now both of us should be heading to the Eielson Air Force base. You will have better access than me. You go to the base and see what you can find and I will spend my time driving around the area. The ancient site is on the edge of the base, which means that part of it may be off the base." Susan said.

"Yeah that covers two birds with one stone. We will let you know what the base personnel have to say. You let us know if you see anything." Rich said.

"Okay talk to you soon." Susan said as she headed toward the rental car area.

A half hour later, on their way to Eielson, Rose turned to Richard with a serious look on her face.

"Do you really think Susan will cooperate with us?"

"The FBI has done some work on her background. As best we can tell, the Chinese government threatened her father's business if she refused to become a spy. Her family faced ruin as her father's import business depended on Chinese goods. China is doing the same thing with other American born Chinese. Susan has never been to China and speaks little or no Cantonese or Mandarin. She tried to escape to Bolivia but the Chinese would not let her go. The whole story is a sad one. Susan is a traitor but she is no lover of China. The CIA and the FBI are considering whether to offer Susan the opportunity to become a double agent but have no done so as yet. So as much as we can trust any spy of a foreign country we can trust her." Rich answered.

"Okay we'll see what happens. As you asked, we had the FBI contact Colonel Madison who runs the base. We've been cleared to enter the base and to see the ancient site. I'm not sure what we will find going to the site. Obviously, Edward and Mary Ann won't just walk up to the site. They would never gain entry. Still, I think we have to cover this base before we go any farther."

An hour later after touring the site, Rich received a phone call. He listened carefully.

"This is Susan. I assume you looked at the Air Force base entrance. I think there is another one. I saw a car by the side of the road close to the Air Force base. I walked directly into the forest where I saw some disturbed bushes. About a hundred yards in, a hole is being dug into the ground. I heard voices down there and saw some dirt being thrown out of the hole. I think Edward and Mary Ann found the other entrance to the site. I have notified my Chinese counterparts of this intelligence. I am notifying you because I have decided to become a double agent. Your FBI offered me the opportunity in return for my services. I'm sending you the GPS location but I don't think you will have any trouble finding it. I must get out of here immediately. My job is done and I don't want my Chinese handlers to become suspicious. Good hunting." Susan said.

"Thank you Susan and good luck to you. I'm sorry that you've been drawn into this whole mess against your will." Rich said as he hung up.

Rich and Rose immediately went to the Colonel's office and asked for some troops to go to the other entrance. He also notified his handlers at the FBI. He didn't know what he could do to stop Edward and Mary Ann but he had to try.

ANCIENT SITE

Jeffrey drove Edward and Mary Ann to the site. As Jeffrey said, the US Air Force guarded the site nearest to the base but had no visible guards on the buried entrance. Edward wondered whether the military had forgotten about the other entrance or decided for other reasons not to guard it. Jeffrey led them to an area with dense underbrush and largely frozen earth.

"Jeffrey we can't move that earth with these shovels. In time, I could devise a device that will heat the earth enough for us to move it but I am not sure I can do so now. Wait a minute. Our shields can throw off heat. Mary Ann come here and place your hand on the frozen earth. I will do the same. Now both of us need to concentrate on melting the earth. The shields are now integrated with our minds. Our shields should respond." Edward said.

As heat flowed from their hands into the ground, the ground slowly became soft enough to dig. Jeffrey dug around the area of Edward and Mary Ann's hands until the ground became soft in the entire area. Then all three of them dug. An hour later, they finally hit something metallic. With some additional hard work, Edward, Mary Ann and Jeffrey uncovered the access door. The door had no lock. With all three of them pulling, the door slowly pulled open. The three explorers descended the stairway in front of them. At the bottom, they saw what must be a door but the smooth door had no hinges, nobs or handles. The door did, however, have an imprint pad for a hand but the hand seemed to have unusually long fingers. Jeffrey spoke.

"We have long believed this to be the entry pad but our hands and hundreds of other items we placed upon it have not worked. Edward you have long fingers, but your fingers appear short by comparison with the imprint pad. Are you ready to try?"

"Yes I think so."

Just at that moment, the three heard the heavy thud of combat boots. Four airman armed with M-16's confronted the trio.

"Get away from that door. You are trespassing on government property."

"Actually, we're not. This entrance is on private land. The other entrance is on government property. I know this. I guarded this facility for many years. My name is Jeffrey."

"Doesn't matter. I have orders to apprehend anyone trying to access this site. If they do not cooperate, I have orders to kill them. I'm going to follow my orders."

"Jeffrey, get behind me." Mary Ann said.

"This is your last chance." The lead airman said.

"I'm sorry we can't do that." Edward said.

At just this moment, Rich and Rose walked forward holding up their hands to prevent the lead airman from firing.

"Wait a minute. Before you fire, I would like to have a few words with Edward and Mary Ann. I'm Richard and this is Rose. In Chicago, the FBI hired us to track you. We have done so ever since. I know a great deal about both of you. I also know that you have personal protective shields that would make this M-16 fire useless. The military has, however, provided me with spent uranium ammunition, which I have provided to the airman. Some military scientists believe this very heavy and slightly radioactive ammunition will penetrate your shields but they have not tested it as yet so they really don't know. In any case, your government does not want you to access the ancient site. They are fearful of what powers you might unleash. They will allow you to enter the site with a team of specially selected people. So we can avoid unnecessary violence if you just come with us. But we must hurry. I saw the Chinese spy who has shadowed us nearby. She will probably call in a Chinese special forces team, who will without doubt have weapons they believe will penetrate your shields."

"I must go to the home world of the advanced race that has provided me with this vast storehouse of knowledge. They and only they will have answers as to why this information has been placed in my DNA. Somehow this all fits into a broader theme of what is happening in the galaxy among races more advanced than our own. For our own good and protection I must find out where we fit into all this. Fighting among ourselves over whatever advanced technology I can provide makes no sense if one of the races providing it suddenly decides to invade or destroy us. If I don't go now I will never go. No nation will want me to leave without first getting this advanced science from me. There is no end to the conflict among nations over who controls me."

When Edward following his remarks took a step toward the keypad, the lead airman opened up with his M 16. His three brothers in arms did likewise. The sound in the small chamber nearly deafened the people without the shields. The bullets bounced off the shields with no effect. A couple of bullets did however, hit Jeffrey, one of the airman and Rose. In all three cases, they received a painful but not life threatening wound in the arm.

The lead airman spoke again.

"That's impossible. We must have fired thirty of these very heavy uranium bullets at you and you remain unharmed except for a ricochet round you took Jeffrey. Yes I know who you are. You worked with my father on this very same base. Bill one of my men also took a ricochet round as did Rose. Who are you?"

"Rose oh my god Rose you are hurt. Airmen stand down." Rich said.

"You need to listen to Richard. Look, these shields can fire a ray that will knock you out for hours. It isn't entirely safe. If you have any kind of heart problem, this stun function can kill you. You have ten seconds." Edward said with a great deal of anger.

The lead airman looked at Edward for several seconds then motioned his men, Rich and Rose to leave. As soon as they disappeared up the stairs, Edward placed his hand on the pad. Almost instantly, the two feet thick door, he had not seen, slid open. Edward, Mary Ann and Jeffrey stepped through the door. Richard suddenly ran down the stairs toward the door but the door closed in his face. The tunnel that lay before Edward, Mary Ann and Jeffrey suddenly showed powerful and multi color lights. They had a clear path forward. Mary Ann spoke to both Jeffrey and Edward with a great deal of concern on her face.

"How badly are you both hurt? I can understand why you are hurt Jeffrey but Edward like me you have the shield. I noticed how you turned away from the lead airman so he couldn't see your injury. I tried to control my emotions but I wanted to run to you Edward."

"Good call Mary Ann. They didn't need to know that their spent uranium munitions had an impact on our shields. If they had, they would have kept firing at us. Fortunately, my shield slowed the bullet down so much it only penetrated my lightweight vest less than a centimeter. Any more penetration and I could have been seriously injured or killed. These shields are designed to ward off minor explosions, energy weapons and regular guns. The Hellfire Missile seriously degraded our shields, allowing these special bullets to penetrated them slightly. I tried to take almost all of the bullets to protect you and Jeffrey. All I need is a little first aid. Where I am going if I get there the aliens can fix my shield. Mary Ann, you need to be careful with your shield. I don't have any tools to fix it here. Jeffrey, how is your injury? It looks like the bullet went right through your arm."

"It did and missed my artery in doing so. I will be okay with a little first aid. But I have no idea how Mary Ann and I are going to get out of this place. The military will arrest us. If they don't the Chinese special forces team will."

"When we walked down here, I began to receive genetic memories. There is a third entrance that goes north and a fourth that goes south. The aliens believe that all structures should have at least four entrances. The entrance to the north appears to be the best of the choices. I will show it to you in a minute. Depending on what happens, three or perhaps two of us will be leaving that way. With the soldiers concentrating on the two known entrances you should be all right. Even if you are caught,

Mary Ann's shield will protect you provided of course she doesn't take a lot of uranium rounds. So maybe I should forget about going on this trip. I don't want Mary Ann hurt or you for that matter Edward."

"Edward and Jeffrey, I'll be fine. You need to take this trip Edward. My reporter's nose tells me that these ancients know things that affect our world. They gave you access to their knowledge for a reason. You have to find out why they left here and what role they plan to play in our future."

"Okay but I will never forgive myself if you are hurt anyway." Edward said.

The trio moved slowly down the long corridor in front of them. The smooth walls showed no items of interest but the group nonetheless marveled at the changing colors swirling around them. After ten minutes, the trio came to another door with a similar keypad. As before the placement of Edward's hand on the board opened the door. This time the trio walked into a control room with a circular ring similar to the one Edward designed for trips back and forth to the solar system's planets and moons. A control panel stood against one wall with writing on it. The writing bore no resemblance to any language on Earth but Edward with his genetic memory could read it. The language provided instructions on how to activate the ring. Edward spoke.

"Now we have a decision to make. I'm probably the only one who should take this trip. I have the genetic memory, which makes me more acceptable to the aliens on the other side of this device. Neither of you have this kind of tie to them. Also, the risk of this trip is great. We have noticed physical strain on travelers who have used my device to go to Mars and the other destinations in the solar system. One older scientist had a heart attack. If I am right, this trip will be much, much longer traveling many light years and thus the strain on our hearts will be much greater. May Ann I love you with all my heart. I don't know what I would do if somehow I made the trip and you did not."

"As much as I would like to go, I can't. My heart is bad. I've already had one attack. If what you say is true, I would die on this journey." Jeffrey said.

"Edward I'm confused. To explain my feelings, first I've a confession to make. After I found out who you really were by reading the article in Discover, I called the Science Advisor to the President. Next to the article on you, he placed an ad encouraging people who might have seen you to call him. I left a message on his recording telling him our story until that point. The Science Advisor called me personally a day later. We had a long conversation where he convinced me to stay with you. I had at this point been thinking of cutting off our relationship. As we both often said, you are not nor were you ever my type. For the good of the country and even the human race, I agreed to do so. I even married you after the Science Advisor convinced me I needed to do so.

"The Science Advisor didn't want the military to control you. He wanted you to further explore what he called your genetic memory. As long as I kept him informed of where we were and what we were doing, he felt satisfied. In turn the Science Advisor warned me when our pursuers came near. Remember how I convinced you to go to Spokane shortly after we arrived at the Montana house. The Science Advisor knew that the FBI closed in on us. When you told me that you had discovered the ancient transport site, the Science Advisor wanted me to encourage you to activate the site and travel to the remote and advanced world of the aliens. I still text the US Science Advisor weekly.

"Still, as I stand here next to you, I don't really want you to go. I guess I love you after all. The problem is really mine, not yours. Because of my beauty and childhood, I have a very difficult time becoming close to anyone. I don't trust men, who constantly are after me. As a result, I think they want to possess my beauty rather than love me. It is much easier when I like a guy to run away from him than to actually invest in a relationship. But I find myself trusting you and believing that you actually love me. Also, you are the only man that I will ever know that will offer me an interesting life not just a safe and wealthy one. I haven't been bored one minute with you. So I guess what I am really saying is that I will go with you if you want or I will stay and wait for you. The choice is yours. That is of course if you forgive me for what I have done."

"May Ann, I'm not surprised by what you just said but I'm very grateful that you told me the truth. I've long suspected that you might not be totally committed to our relationship, but I've had no ability to call you on it. I just love you too much. The fact that you really do love me after all makes me very happy despite your betrayal of me. Yet, as I have already said I don't want you to make the trip. If you lost your life as a result of the trip, I would probably take my own. Also, I need you to keep our lives going here so we can begin them again when I return. You are my connection to this world. Now, I need you to protect Jeffrey with your shield at least until Jeffrey can make it home. I will miss you every moment of every day, but I believe it is my destiny to take this trip. Now let's find the way for you to get out and return so I can make the trip."

After the trio established their escape route, they returned to the room where the ring stood. Edward closely followed the directions until the ring suddenly came alive. Edward could not find any instructions on how to point the device in any particular direction. The destination seemed preset. The side of the ring contained another hand pad similar to the ones he had already activated.

Edward placed his hand on the keypad next to the ring and watched the area inside of the ring change. The ring swiveled backwards toward the ceiling. A door in the ceiling opened and blew a hole in the dirt to the surface. Edward turned to Mary Ann and Jeffrey.

"My time has come. Mary Ann please know that I will love you until the end of time and that I will return to you. If I'm able, I will come back within 6 months. Jeffrey thanks for helping us. I hope our government is not too hard on you."

"They will find out what I know but in the end I will be of little further use to them. As a former service member I will probably be all right. I will check up on Mary Ann from time to time to make sure she is doing well. Now go."

Edward climbed up a stairway into the ring, took one last look at Mary Ann and disappeared. Immediately after he left, the door above them slid closed and the dirt pushed to one side fell into the hole that had been made. Mary Ann and Jeffrey left on their northern escape route. When everyone had departed, the facility fell into darkness awaiting the next user.

REUNION

Edward stared at his reflection in a mirror. The Knowldon had made him unrecognizable. Mary Ann wouldn't know it to be him until Edward revealed to her their magic word, Neanderthal, that he agreed to say to her when he returned. Unknown to anyone, Edward purchased before he left Earth a second small house in Anchorage and stocked the home with clothes, new identification and large amounts of money. He came back through the air force base portal from where he left. He used the same north entrance that Jeffrey and Mary did to leave the facility. To his knowledge no one detected his arrival. Edward's grander home in Anchorage might very well be watched. In the six months he stayed in the Knowldon Home World, anything could have happened to his wife. Without Edward there to protect her, Mary Ann might work more closely for the government than she already had cooperating with the Science Advisor. She might be with another man. She had betrayed his trust once. Mary Ann could do it again.

The trip from the Air Force Base, after he journeyed back to Earth, went very well. Now possessed of all the Knowldon's vast technological and scientific knowledge, Edward used his invisibility device attached to his personal shield to simply walk down the road until he reached a small restaurant. He then commandeered a car and drove to his small home. His shield started the car with only a thought from Edward. Edward debated in his mind whether to call Jeffrey but he wanted to maintain as much invisibility as he could. Calling Jeffrey would risk his detection. Also, the government might be watching his place after Edward's escape.

Edward parked the car several blocks away from his house and only exited it when no one watched and as an invisible man. Wearing gloves from the time he first approached the car, Edward left no fingerprints. He hoped the shocked diner he saw when he drove away would find his car soon. The man still had the keys. Edward entered the small home through the back door. In the short time he had been in the house, Edward already booked a flight to Chicago. Mary Ann would most likely be at their home there.

Edward had only one reason to return to Earth, Mary Ann. He thought of her everyday. Edward had to return to her. The Knowldon, who looked a little like human beings but stood taller with very high foreheads, wanted him to stay and become a part of their world. According to the Knowldon, their ancestors started the human line hundreds of thousands of years ago from an ancestor of both humans and Neanderthals and thus had a great interest in their experiment and how it turned out in people like Edward. At the same time, they recognized the threat Earth would soon face from their fierce and violent rivals, the Razeurs. With his new knowledge, Edward could help the people of Earth better defend themselves against this technologically advanced race. The Razeurs conquered inhabited worlds by killing all sentient beings there with a few exceptions made for the most brilliant scientists and other stragglers they turned into slaves. They used specially designed viruses deadly only to the host race like humans in this case, neutron bombs and powerful pulse canons to eliminate their prey.

Edward traveled to Chicago with little fear of discovery. His DNA and fingerprints differed as much as his appearance, but in truth he had the same memories, personality and feelings as before. After returning to Chicago, he visited an Internet café and spent many hours reading news reports from the last 6 months. The news astounded him. Before he left, Edward reset the lasers he had provided the military so they would work well in his absence but had turned them off for a month to retaliate for the Hell Fire Missile attack. He only restored them because a geologist friend called him about a foreign nuclear threat to the Yellowstone Super Volcano. Apparently, the military contacted his friend with detailed questions about how a nuclear detonation would affect the rock dome that kept the Super Volcano from erupting. Edward knew such an eruption would almost destroy the US and greatly harm the rest of the world. Mary Ann would almost certainly die in such an attack. Edward just couldn't let this happen.

In his absence, this threat to Yellowstone became real. North Korea launched an ICBM toward Yellowstone with a powerful 50-megaton bomb. They operated on the mistaken information that the advanced lasers and shields he provided the American military no longer worked. The military then used his lasers to destroy not only this missile threat but every ICBM in Russia, North Korea and China in addition to destroying the missile. When these countries threatened war over the destruction, the U.S. threatened to destroy every major offensive weapon owned by these countries. The situation quickly cooled and the war threat disappeared. Edward could not believe that his weapons which he hated creating actually prevented war.

After reading the history of the last 6 months, Edward looked for signs of Mary Ann on the Internet. A recent article in the Chicago Tribune said that the wife of the famous scientist had rejoined her old PR firm and taken up residence in their Chicago apartment in the wake of Edward's mysterious absence. Edward knew her schedule. He would intercept Mary Ann on her way to work. Edward decided this approach would work best. If the government did have control of her or at least her communications, a phone call warning Mary Ann of his presence could result in a major military and police force welcome. If they were to spend any time together, she would have to agree to keep his real identity secret.

Edward waited anxiously near the bus stop by the high rise they both occupied. With his new appearance, Edward did not want to just show up at the condo. Mary Ann liked to take a bus, near her condo, which took Mary Ann very close to her office. He arrived at 7 a.m. She usually boarded the bus between 7 and 8 am depending on how late she worked the night before. At 7:15, Edward saw her approaching. She did not have a man with her, which greatly lightened Edward's heart.

Edward promised to return in 6 months but in truth he had no idea when he left whether he would return let alone in this time period. Edward walked casually toward her. When they drew close, he said with a big smile and a strong voice.

"Neanderthal."

Mary Ann stopped and stared at Edward for several moments without saying anything. Before she could speak, Edward talked.

"Mary Ann, I know that I do not look the same as I did, but I assure you I am the same Edward who married you. The Knowldon altered me in a way that no one on this planet would recognize me. This gives us a chance to live a life without outside interference, a life filled with music. I tried to create a look that you would like, but still had enough of the real me in it so I could be the person I once was. I can see by your reaction that you are not pleased to see me."

Mary Ann finally spoke.

"Even though you met your 6 month deadline, I didn't expect to see you again. I have to say your timing is great. I just started speaking with the many boys after me, but I haven't dated any of them. I swore that I wouldn't until the 6 months expired. I'm glad I waited. Truth is I'm glad to see you. I missed our adventures. I missed being with the smartest man in the world. It will, however, take a little while to get used to the new you. By the way, you're better looking."

"Mary Ann I planned for us to be together and make music but events that will take place for Earth in the near future will make this fantasy impossible. An aggressive and murderous race as advanced as the Knowldon, the Razeurs plan on invading Earth in the near future. Earth will have no chance against them. Even though a Knowldon treaty with the Razeurs permits this invasion in our year 2023, the Knowldon allowed me access to all their knowledge and technology so I could return and mount a defense. I will need to begin building these defenses as soon as possible. The weapons we will need will be very hard to build and very expensive. I need to appear before the United Nations and make my case. Do you still have your personal shield?"

"No they drugged me one night and kept me in jail until I let them remove it. When they did, of course, the shield self-destructed. They made all sorts of threats but the Science Advisor persuaded them that if you ever returned, they would need me to make you cooperate. Keeping me in jail would not win your cooperation but rather your hate. They finally let me go. I should have used the power of the shield to prevent them from taking me in the first place."

"That's okay. As long as you are not hurt, we can go on. I will install a new more powerful shield on you. This shield has more offensive capabilities than the last. We will use the Science Advisor as the means to gain access to the UN. Getting the world to cooperate will be very difficult and take more time than it should. If at the end of the day, the world will not cooperate, you and I will have to go to Knowldon. I know now that you will be well treated there. We will be able to live our lives. Yet, right now, I have a request. Call in sick to work. I need to have you in my arms."

"I think we can arrange that. We have six months of catching up to do. As I stand here looking at the real you through your eyes, I am reminded of the love we have."

AN INTIMATE NIGHT

After making love to Mary Ann, Edward turned to her. "Mary Ann, I need to share a little more of what happened on Knowldon. When I arrived, the Knowldon regarded me as a curiosity. Although the Knowldon live a long time, no living person in the community had any personal experience with humans. The scientific community, however, had an interest in how I inherited only a partial genetic memory from my parents who had been exposed to the memory gas, the Knowldon left on Earth. After conducting many tests, they realized I possessed a great scientific mind. For this reason, they made the alterations in my DNA needed to give me the full genetic memory possessed by the Knowldon population. With this new knowledge, I began to work on very advanced Knowldon scientific projects. Of course, I could communicate with the Knowldon as I possessed their genetic memories. One of the scientists who worked for the Knowldon military, Trill, became a good and close friend. He helped me navigate the Knowldon culture and cheered me up when I became depressed over your absence."

"While slowly making some friends and colleagues in the scientific community, the general population and the rulers of this world showed little interest in me until I spoke of music. While the Knowldon understand music and its mathematical origins, they showed no aptitude for making music themselves. Their attempts at creating music turned into rigid sharp mathematical tones that they didn't even like very much themselves.

"Knowing that my musical talents might make an impression on the Knowldon, I used their incredible 3d construction programs to fashion a guitar, a piano and a violin. I produced many prototypes until finally

I made instruments that rivaled the best on Earth. Once I had the instruments, I persuaded the Knowldon to attend a concert in one of their capital city's largest auditoriums. Thousands of curious Knowldon decided to attend. For two hours, I played all forms of our music from classical to pop to blues to jazz, utilizing all three of the instruments. I even sang when the song demanded it. The Knowldon fell in love with the music. In particular, they loved my violin playing.

"Following my concert, I received hours of questioning about the music played on our world. I told them millions of humans produced and performed wonderful music. I just played a few pieces for them. Of course, the Knowldon demanded I play for them almost every evening. When I performed, even in their largest stadium, the tickets quickly disappeared. Every time I performed all I could think of is having you by my side. I soon developed a plan to come back here and take you to the Knowldon home world. When the Knowldon learned that you too had musical talent, they strongly endorsed the idea.

"Yet days before I planned on leaving, the Knowldon told me of the Razeurs and their plans for Earth. Technically this information lay in my genetic memory but having the memories and accessing them proved to be very different things. The Knowldon spend their whole lives learning how to do this. I proved to be very much an amateur in retrieving my genetic memory. With this knowledge and some information on the latest Knowldon weapons and shield systems provided to me. I came here to be with you and to face the Razeur threat rather than coming back to take you to Knowldon. The Knowldon wished me well but said they couldn't help us any more than they had."

"I wish I had been there with you Edward. I would have loved making music with you. So what do we do now? The world will not be easy to sell on the threat." Mary Ann said.

"I know but I have to try. At the end of the day, if we fail to persuade them, we can always go to the Knowldon world and perform the rest of our lives. I hope this does not happen but we can only do so much as one man and one woman."

"Edward I truly hope they will listen but I have my doubts."

WORLD COMMUNITY

As predicted, the world community did not warm to the idea of a world-wide effort to combat an unknown foe. Because of Edward's weapons, the balance of power in the world had been disturbed. North Korea's, China's and Russia's actions which led to the unbalance, created many suspicions as well. To gain leverage, Edward stayed out of sight. No one knew what he looked like and as long as this remained true he had the freedom to operate. Also, to gain leverage, Edward once again disabled America's lasers and shields. Edward insisted that he would not enable these weapons again until Edward had the opportunity to speak to the UN. Two precious months passed before a meeting finally came to pass, largely as a result of American pressure on the body. On the day of the meeting, Edward still had not revealed himself to the world. The Science Advisor through some friends arranged for him to gain access to the UN building and the assembly meeting. Finally, Kang the new Secretary General, called for Edward to take the stage even though he had no idea where Edward might be.

Edward on cue walked to the podium and began the speech he hoped would lead them to a program to stop the Razeurs. Edward appeared as the Edward who had left America, not the way he looked now. His shield could change his facial appearance at will. Edward would leave the UN as a young computer technician Sam Young. He already had this likeness programed into his shield and forged documents that would let him leave the UN after his speech. Edward did not trust any of the UN governments including his own. The guards near the podium patted him down before allowing him to take the stage. Edward stared at his audience for a full minute before beginning.

"My story begins three thousand years ago. Two great empires inhabit this part of the galaxy: the Knowldon and the Razeurs. Their technology mirrors what you have seen in science fiction pictures like Star Trek and Star Wars. Like all empires, they have both pursued expansion. The Knowldon prefer to persuade worlds to join their own while the Razeurs take worlds by force, often destroying sentient beings in the process. The Knowldon and the Razeurs have over the millennia negotiated several treaties. They have also fought wars, which have never resulted in the rewards the different sides hoped they would achieve. The Knowldon discovered Earth first. A beautiful planet, Earth represented a major prize. As their custom, the Knowldon developed some bases and started their very slow process of colonization. When the Razeurs learned of Earth, they objected very forcefully to Knowldon colonization. Earth lies closer to the Razeur home world and the Knowldon undertook the last major colonization of a beautiful world like Earth at this point in time. War seemed imminent, but at the last moment, a treaty agreement emerged. The Knowldon would immediately evacuate Earth, the Earth would remain un-colonized for 3000 years and at the end of this time, 2023 on our calendar, the Razeurs would become the empire to colonize the planet. When the Razeurs colonized earth, they would not destroy the native sentient species. No one expected the Razeurs to honor this part of the treaty. Their record shows annihilation of a sentient native species when they colonize a planet. Yet, for the last 3000 years, the other parts of the treaty held.

"When the Knowldon evacuated Earth, they left some transport sites like the one at Eielson Air Force base in Alaska, which could be activated to send Knowldons to Earth or Earthlings to Knowldon. They also left some pods with a special DNA altering gas. When activated the gas causes genetic mutations in humans that could allow future generations to develop the Knowldon genetic memory. The Knowldon, while not more intelligent than humans, have the unique ability to pass on all their knowledge to offspring through this genetic memory process. My father a scientist at Eielson and my mother a technician in the same lab activated one of these pods and breathed in the gas. As a result, I received some of the genetic memories of the Knowldon. This has enabled me to develop the advanced technology you have seen such as the machine I developed to transport people instantly to other planets in the solar system. The US has used this machine to colonize Mars, Ganymede, Europa, Titan and our Moon. In addition, expeditions have been sent to other moons and planets. Also, as many of you are aware, I developed some powerful lasers and defense shields which the US military has used.

"While I had some of the Knowldon memory, I did not have it all. So, I used the Eielson ancient site to journey to Knowldon, where I did receive the full Knowldon memory. I could use this site because the Knowldon machines recognized me as a Knowldon. Also, on the Knowldon home world, I received special information on the latest Knowldon military technology. The Knowldon are unhappy about what Earth faces in 2023 and wanted us to be able to develop some weapons that might help us resist a Razeur attempt to obliterate us. I would like to develop this technology with all of Earth through the United Nations. I no longer have any desire to work solely with the US military. They have attempted to murder me with a Hell Fire missile, a MOAB II bomb and machine gun fire. If you chose not to work with me, I will return to the Knowldon Home World and allow Earth to deal with the Razeurs using your primitive weapons. The choice is yours."

At first, Edward's remarks were met with silence; then the questions came. The questions lasted for hours. Basically, no one seemed to trust anyone else. The UN representatives agreed something had to be done but couldn't think of how to do it. They all worried that one country would use the advanced technology developed against other countries they deemed undesirable. Finally, the diplomats of the world, who could not negotiate the annihilation of the human race, turned the decisions on how to proceed over to the scientists of the world. They would back them through the World Bank with the funds they needed. Edward had the last word.

"Everyday we delay, we begin digging our own graves. The Razeurs don't negotiate, they eliminate. You can't reason with them. They won't listen. They consider us primitive by comparison. They see no reason for our species to exist when they can propagate their own on our world. We must begin now."

Edward quickly turned away after leaving the podium. Burying himself in the crowd that developed, Edward changed his appearance to Sam Young. As the crowd searched for Edward, he quietly walked out of the main assembly room and made his way to the front door. The UN police carefully examined his credentials before they allowed him to continue. As he exited the building, Edward noticed a large collection of military vehicles and police cars. The officers in front of the building carefully examined him a second time before allowing him to continue on his way. They even gathered a DNA sample from him, which they instantly checked. Since the Knowldon altered his DNA, the test came out negative for Isaac. Edward would return to Alaska where he hoped Mary Ann still waited for him. As he fully expected, the next years would not be easy ones for him or Mary Ann.

THE PURSUERS AGAIN.

Rich and Rose spent months in the Anchorage area looking for Mary Ann's and Edward's house. They found no trace of it despite searching the lands held by small corporations. Edward held his land this way but for whatever reason, the corporations they thought most likely to be his held only empty land. A very tired Rich complained about their failed efforts.

"This like looking for a needle in a haystack. Edward's house is hidden but how I don't know. We have looked in every valley and secluded spot in this area.'

"As your devoted assistant and wife, I usually come up with an idea but I don't have one this time. Alaska is huge. When we start expanding the area beyond Eielson, the target area becomes almost too large to search. The mountainous areas are particularly hard to scan. Despite all this, I expect something else is going on here."

"Like what?" Rich asked.

"You forget that Edward now has the Knowldon's full genetic memory and thus assess to technology we can't even imagine. I read a little sci fi when I was younger. His property might be cloaked. I know it sounds far fetched but it would explain our inability to see his house."

"That is far fetched but if it were true how would we find it?"

"We could walk some of the more likely parcels. This could involve hundreds of miles of walking depending on when we ran into one of his shields. We could use drones to help reduce the walking."

'You might have something there. I guess we could ask our handlers and see what they say."

"Not just do it on our own?"

"Rose I will be honest with you. I'm not sure I want to find his house. What if Edward is correct and this aggressive race shows up in a few years. Edward is our only way of defending against these reportedly nasty beings. If the US captures Edward and tries to control him, the rest of the nations of the world will stop cooperating. All the preparations to date could cease as nations fight over their own security. I don't want either of us to die from a nasty virus or from a neutron bomb. I want to live. To be quite honest with you, the US has treated Edward and Mary Ann poorly. I'm not sure I want the US to start attacking Edward and Mary Ann's new home the way they did their Montana home. Twice now we have vowed to stop this search but in both cases we continued the search."

"Okay why don't we do this? We will tell the FBI we think Edward's home is hidden by cloaking technology and ask if we can follow this theory. If the FBI says yes, we will do so, but if we are fortunate enough to find the home, we will then decide if we want to tell anyone about it. If they say no we will quit the project. This will keep us in the game and give us some control over what happens. I have long suspected that the FBI has hired other people like us. Who is to say that these other searchers haven't thought of the same thing?" Rose said.

"Yeah that makes sense. I'm glad I have such a smart wife. We will begin our search provided the FBI says okay." Rich responded.

THE MID POINT.

After four long years, a very tired Edward spent some time with Mary Ann. Since appearing before the United Nations, Edward worked almost everyday to build the weapons they needed to build. During this time, he and Mary Ann had to keep there whereabouts hidden. The US as well as other large nations still hunted them. Nonetheless, ten giant pulse weapons, which required the building of huge reactor for each, now stood at the ready in separate locations around the globe. Each pulse gun had a powerful shield surrounding it. Also, thousands of nuclear mines surrounded the planet. With Knowlton technology upgrades, the mines had very effective cloaks and a design that focused most of the explosion in one direction, thereby increasing the amount of explosive power focused on the enemies shields. These revolutionary mines could be silently moved close to Razeur ships before exploding. Edward had no idea whether these powerful weapons would be enough to counter the firepower the Razeurs would bring. He spoke to Mary Ann.

"Mary Ann I've tried. The Razeurs will be here in approximately 9 months. You've done a great job along with your fellow PR professionals of promoting our project. The whole world is invested in this. The political difficulties in getting to this place have been enormous. On two occasions both of us wanted to quit and go to the Knowldon home world. Yet at the end of the day, we all need to survive. This is all we are trying to do. I even think the Knowldon would be proud of us."

"Yes I've been happy to do my part albeit in a way that keeps my location and identity secret but without you Earth would be defenseless.

The work and achievements of billions of people over several hundred thousand years would be gone, lost to history. I hope we've learned our lesson. At the end of the day, despite all the threats, posturing, murder and mayhem in our world, we are all humans and have contributed much to this world and have much to contribute to other worlds. Other races are in competition with us for the space we occupy. We either fight them for it or perish. If we win, will the fight be over?" Mary Ann said.

"No probably not. From what I know of the Razeurs from the Knowldon, they do not know or recognize defeat. They will come after us again. But what we will have won is their respect. Maybe we can convince them that the human race should survive in this galaxy. Yet this is a discussion for another day. First we have to win this battle. The number one thing we will have going for us is the Knowldon belief that we have a relative primitive society. They won't be expecting cloaked self-propelled fusion mines and giant pulse canons and as a result I hope will not be prepared. Of course, if they come a second time, they will be prepared." Edward answered.

"You really think we will win at least this time?"

"Yes but there will be a cost. I expect the Razeurs to come at us aggressively. We will take damage. For this reason alone, I hope they never come but of course they will. But honestly what I would like to do right now is to fly to our vacation home in Montana and wait together for the fight that will come. This fourth house we bought in Northern Wisconsin doesn't really have what the Montana and Alaska houses have. Both of us can communicate with everyone that needs us in Montana. We probably need to move again anyway. If the fight goes poorly, I would like to spend my last days with you in a place unique to us."

"Okay. I would like that, but aren't you going to escape to the Knowldon home world if we are losing? You are still the only one that can access the ancient site."

"First and foremost, I would never leave you again. You would have to go with me. Second, I don't know whether I could live with myself abandoning my race and Earth. The two of us would be some kind of curiosity in Knowldon, the forgotten race of humans. But I have never asked you how you feel. We've just been too busy."

"I don't know. I would go if you go but I feel pretty much the same way about it you do. If we change our mind, we should probably go to the Alaska home instead so we are close to the ancient site. It's almost as nice as the Montana place."

"Okay Mary Ann, we will do that. One of the pulse canons is in Alaska. We will be close to at least some of the action when the time comes. We'll take a flight up there tomorrow."

THE LONG PROCESS

6 months later, Edward shut down his computer after another very long and difficult day. Edward spent a great deal of time resolving the technical problems at the Alaska pulse canon site as well as the pulse canon sites in the rest of the world. The balance of the day he spent working on the space mine technology. He accomplished all of this through his elaborate computer system. Mary Ann who had been appointed the spokesperson for the project spent countless hours trying to settle disputes among the nations. They constantly fought over the cost overruns and the control of the technology. They spent most of their time trying to figure out who would control the technology after the Razeurs came if they ever did. Mary like Edward had to do this from the Alaska site to shield their location from the world. Mary Ann greeted Edward after both had spent many hours working on their projects.

"Hello darling. You look as tired as I feel. I think most of our partners don't believe in the Razeurs. They merely agreed to participate to gain access to your technology. This is particularly true with the smaller nations who fear that this technology will be used to dominate them. The closer we get to the actual deployment of these weapons the fiercer the fights become. At any given time, I have at least two nations boycotting the UN effort. I'm surprised the whole thing hasn't fallen apart. I've largely kept this from you. You after all must develop and build the weapons, but I need to share it with you now. I may go crazy if I don't."

"I suspected you endured this endless bad behavior from our nation supporters. I often receive second hand knowledge of it. This is why we must keep our location secret. I fear they would still try to capture and dominate us. Although I suspect as the worlds nations become more committed to the project their desire to capture us will decline. Unknown to the nations of the world, I have buried self-destruct software into all of the technology that has been built. If one or more nations try to use these weapons against some other Earth nation the weapons will cease to operate. The important thing is that the weapons are coming along nicely. We will test this one in Alaska next week. As to the mines, we have used 2000 nuclear warheads from our world's nuclear powers as the basis of the mine weapons. They fit well inside the Knowldon designed self -propelled cloaked mines and because we made them will be less recognizable to the Razeurs. Once they reach a proximity to the alien ships where they can be effective, they will be triggered by any scan from the alien ships. If any of the mines reach the enemy's shields without being targeted, they will detonate. Obviously the closer the mines come to the alien ships the more effective they will be. Yet once they are scanned, the aliens will destroy them seconds later. We already have 1800 of the mines produced. All their tests are so far successful. For the first time since we started this project I am beginning to believe we can mount a good defense of our planet, but of course we will not know until their ships finally arrive and we test our defenses in actual combat. I am telling you this because your efforts to keep Earth's nations together and focused on the project are critical to our success. If too may nations leave our Razeur project, we won't be able to produce enough weapons to win."

"Edward we both know what we must do. We just have to do our best. According to your estimates in 3 months they will arrive. Now let's enjoy a meal with a little wine. I have turned off my cell phone. You need to do the same."

"We think alike. I have already turned off my phone. We will enjoy each other's company for an hour or two and then return to the grind.

For two hours, I can just think what it will be like to spend all my time with you."

"I will be thinking the same thing." Mary Ann said.

As Mary Ann and Edward spoke, a very exhausted Rich and Rose flew their tenth drone in a large field 50 miles Northeast of Eielson. Finding Edward's home proved to be more difficult and time consuming than anyone thought. The drone moved about a thousand yards in the distance when it suddenly crashed into an unseen wall. Rose spoke first.

"That must be the shield. Well we finally found it. Now what do we do? From what I read in the paper, this alien race the Razeurs I think they call them will be here in only 3 months. If we tell our FBI handlers will they attack this location?"

"I almost wished we wouldn't find them. As to what our government will do, I haven't a clue. They might very well do nothing until after the Razeurs are expected to arrive were it not for the fact that so many other nations are also looking for Mary Ann and Edward. Our government will worry that if it doesn't control Mary Ann and Edward as soon as they can someone else will. I haven't seen our Chinese friend for almost a month but she is undoubtedly out there somewhere. I expect spies from all the major nations on Earth are also out there. If our government decides to attack Edward's house, the US might actually use the Alaska Pulse Canon Edward developed to destroy the shield surrounding his house. Who knows what kinds of weapons the other countries will use?"

"I have a suggestion. We have the shield location. Let's pretend we found nothing and continue our exploration elsewhere. The other nations watching us will assume we didn't find anything here and will avoid the area. Instead of reporting this to the FBI we will call Science Advisor Rothschild and talk to him about what should be done. He may be the only sane senior official to whom we can reveal this information."

"Rose I like your approach. I would like the Science Advisor's take on all this before we reveal anything to our handlers."

THE RAZEURS

First Rank Admiral Blaze piloted his brand new Omar class Battleship, the Terminator at the head of his four-ship attack formation. The massive 90 kilometer long ship contained 500 attack fighters and over twenty pulse canons including a super pulse canon based on new technology. His other three ships came from the Kamar Class, a smaller 50-kilometer long battleship with 12 pulse canons, 250 fighters and one heavy pulse canon, with almost the same power as one of the regular pulse canons on the Terminator. Admiral Blaze had to lobby very hard for the forces he had. As a first rank admiral, Blaze could lay claim to one of the Omar class ships but most people on the war council felt that this single ship could easily annihilate the human race. They saw no need for the additional ships.

The Razeurs always underwent an analysis of their enemies' capabilities. According to their analysis, which was based on a 15 year-old clandestine trip to the human world, the humans had primitive nuclear weapons but with no ability to deliver them to one of the Razeur ships orbiting Earth. Their chemically based missiles with nuclear warheads and their chemically powered planes, the Razeurs could easily detect and shoot down. This study didn't even find laser-based weapons of any sophistication let alone the advanced pulse based weapons used by the Razeurs.

Admiral Blaze remembered the abduction of the humans well. At the time as a young officer, he commanded the unit in charge. Razeur scientists subjected the humans to many long tests. They needed to engineer a virus that would defeat the humans' defense mechanisms. While this took place, then Lieutenant Blaze conducted a number of torture tests to assess the human captive's abilities to tolerate both physical and psychological pain. Lieutenant Blaze felt that this information would prove to be invaluable in dealing with the small numbers of humans remaining after their near extermination took place. Office Blaze cared little as to whether the subjects lived or died. While the protocol allowed him to return the human subjects to Earth once they had been subjected to all the tests, Officer Blaze decided to keep the human subjects until they perished under his various tortures or from the test viruses. In all 100 humans died at his hands, only a tiny number compared to the billions who would die with the Razeur invasion. Blaze finished the process without developing much respect for the human's tolerance of torture. Razeurs showed a much higher resistance.

Nonetheless, Blaze didn't want to leave anything to chance. With his considerable influence, Blaze managed to convince the war council to provide three Kamar class vessels, which the Razeurs intended to phase out and replace over the next three decades with the Omar vessels. Admiral Blaze knew all too well that wars often provided surprises. With his career on the line, Blaze didn't want to take any chances of failure no matter how small those chances might be.

Omar's four-vessel armada dropped out of hyperspace between the orbits of Earth and Mars. Admiral Blaze immediately ordered the formation of the standard Razeur wedge, the Terminator at the front flanked by two ships on his right and left and one at this back. When the formation reached an orbit position, they would immediately begin firing their weapons at the major targets on the planet: all major cities and military bases of any kind. They would also launch the 1000 advanced tactical fighters to increase their attack effectiveness. The Razeurs did not waste time negotiating with a weak enemy. The major cities would receive enough fire to cripple them but the bases would be annihilated. After all resistance ceased, the one thousand containers with viruses deadly to humans but harmless to Razeurs, would be sent Earthward. The fighters would provide cover for them. If the viruses proved to be only partially effective, neutron bombs would be deployed to further reduce the human population. When the human population declined to token levels, the Razeurs would deploy ships to take over the primitive infrastructure on the planet and begin to modify it to Razeur liking. The Razeurs preferred a warm moist climate. They did not like dry or cold places. As the admiral in charge of the invasion, he would have his pick of palaces on this planet. According to his intelligence, the humans had many magnificent ones from which to pick.

When his vessels orbited Earth, Admiral Blaze calmly ordered the firing to begin and the fighters prepared for launch. Without shields on any of the cities or military facilities, only the pulse canons had shields, the effect of the Razeur barrage could be felt immediately. Yet, only an hour into the attack and before the first fighter departed, Captain Blast approached his admiral with concern all over his face. He actually turned red, a sign of extreme stress.

"Admiral I just started receiving strange images on our sensors. After I asked our other ships to alter their sensors to the frequency I am using, they obtained the same images. They are increasing in number. They appear to be heavily cloaked. I'm also showing very powerful energy readings from ten places on the planet. I'm focusing our more powerful pulse canons on these readings, but unlike the other sites they have powerful shields. Admiral. . ."

"Idiot!! It's a classical Konwldon space mine/pulse attack. You. . ..

At just this moment, the world outside the Razeur ships turned into a sun like brilliance as over two thousand shaped hydrogen fusion bombs detonated around the Razeur ships. The Razeur vessels identified many of the mines before they came dangerously close but as soon as they did, the mines exploded. Some mines even made it to the Razeur shields before exploding. The cumulative effect of so many powerful nuclear warheads exploding badly damaged the shields of all the Razeur ships. As the launch doors had already opened for the fighters, the damaged shields allowed powerful surges of energy to penetrate the ships. These ships might have still survived but seconds later six very powerful pulses hit the damaged Razeur vessels. The three Kamar class ships exploded violently after receiving the pulse blasts. The Terminator, the finest war ship ever produced by the Razeurs, did not explode but barely hung together after the attack. Admiral Blaze had been thrown from one part of the bridge to another still strapped to his chair. Fires broke out everywhere. Red screens flashed in the smoke. Admiral Blaze had no shields, no weapons and no propulsion. His launch bay area received so much damage that the massive ship barely hung together. Most of the Razeurs on the bridge with him lay dead.

As his head cleared, Admiral Blaze realized he had no options. Another pulse from the Earth based guns would destroy him and his ship before his shields and weapons could be restored. He thought about crashing his massive ship into the planet to cause more damage to Earth but by the time he or what he could find of his crew restored propulsion, another Earth pulse canon would destroy his ship. The admiral needed a miracle but he had no time to produce one. His long held adage of never underestimating the enemy came to him as another massive pulse blast turned his world into an inferno.

SCIENCE ADVISOR

Science Advisor Terry Rothschild breathed a sigh of relief when the Razeurs finally arrived. For the last 3 months, he hid the whereabouts of Edward's home from his government. When the two FBI contractors called him with the information, he persuaded them to keep it to themselves and to mislead any foreign governments who came near the location. The misleading part became an almost full time job for Rich and Rose and for him as well. They constantly left breadcrumbs of information for all these governments to find that led them in the wrong direction. The Science Advisor had long ago identified his leaks and used them extensively to feed the misinformation effort. He expected to be fired and arrested almost every day. Rich and Rose expected the same. Yet at the end of the day, Terry never doubted his decision. Terry knew the Razeur would come for his nation and his world. They had to be stopped. It was a matter of survival.

On the day before the Razeur expected arrival, the Science Advisor had to manage a major crisis when the whereabouts of Edward and Mary Ann's house became known. Rich and Rose felt they could no longer keep the information secret and reported it to their FBI handlers before the Razeurs would arrive. If they waited, they both exposed themselves to arrest and possibly prosecution. The Science Advisor reluctantly agreed that this was the right course of action to protect both of them.

As in Montana, General Porter arrived at the location discovered by Rich and Rose but instead of attacking Edward's home he had to defend against Special Forces teams from 10 nations. The information on the whereabouts of Edward Rich and Rose provided the FBI leaked almost immediately. All sorts of exotic weapons appeared on the site including several different types of lasers, sonic projectors, and a variety of guns with uranium ammunition. General Porter fought through the night into the next day with these groups. When the Razeurs made their presence known, the various teams suddenly stopped fighting. The General did as well. Despite their personal desire to fight onward, the US and all the Special Forces soldiers' governments ordered them to withdraw. Not a single experimental weapon fired upon Edward's shield. The military forces of the world had a new enemy. A hundred soldiers died in what now seemed a fruitless operation.

Fear suddenly gripped the Science Advisor. His moment of relief for making it three months without discovery and then the withdrawal of forces around Edward's house gave way to the realization that a very advanced alien race as murderous as Stalin or Hitler came for them. Better than most people, he knew how terrible their weapons would be. Terry decided he would spend the day at his synagogue. He needed to be close to his god if the day did not go well.

THE HUMAN SIDE

The military operations outside Edward's Alaska home shield proved to be no more than a distraction. By the time this all started, the weapons systems designed to fight the Razeurs had already been brought to full readiness. If they lost the battle to come, no one would care about him and his special knowledge. If they won, they would need his cooperation for the next battle. The Razeurs only brought four large ships this time. If they lost, they would bring many more the next time. Still Edward bristled a little at the constant attacks on him and more importantly his wife. The nations of the world made it very hard for him to save the human race they represented. Edward with some effort pushed these thoughts out of his mind and concentrated on the task ahead.

Edward connected with the 10 military commanders around the world, who would fight the Razeurs appearing above their world. He would consult with them as to when the fusion mines would be detonated and the massive pulse cannons fired seconds later. The Knowldon had found this to be an effective strategy against the Razeurs when they did not suspect superior weaponry on a planet or moon. As soon as the Razeurs began firing on Earth, many of the commanders wanted to respond immediately. Chen of China led the chorus.

"We must respond immediately. Shanghai just received a powerful pulse blast. Millions are dead. The center of the city is destroyed."

Edward replied with an even tone.

"The more fusion mines we can place close to the Razeur ships the better chance we have of disabling their shields for the pulse attack.

Every minute twelve more mines move into position. Shields are designed to recover. If we don't annihilate these ships the first time, we will face an all out attack, which will probably include the launch of a thousand or more fighters. Also, the Razeurs will quickly target and destroy our mines. With our mines gone, our next pulse attack could encounter partially restored shields. The battle could quickly turn in the Razeur's favor. We will know when to attack when our pulse guns or mines are scanned. Then we must attack. The Razeurs will quickly discern what we are doing and move to counter it. This is right out of the Knowldon war book. They have fought the Razeurs many times. They know what works."

"I disagree. You are not a military man. You're a scientist. This decision is for military men. If we don't attack now, the Razeurs will destroy our mines and pulse canons leaving us helpless. I say we put it to a vote." Chen responded.

The discussion continued for several more minutes then the question went to a vote before ten solemn men. The vote came out as a 5 to 5 tie. A minute passed with the ten men not knowing what to do next. Just as Chen rose to speak again, Edward received feedback that both the fusion mines and pulse canons had been scanned.

He calmly said.

"Detonate all the mines and fire the pulse canons. We are being scanned. The Razeurs will soon destroy them." The ten men said simply "agreed."

As the mines detonated and the pulse canons fired thereafter silence descended on the call. After two of the pulse canons fired, they in turn received heavy Razeur fire rendering them inoperable. The Razeurs also destroyed the other pulse canons that had participated in the fight. The generals and Edward saw the losses on their computer screens. The detonation of the mines made it difficult to discern what took place in space. The explosions filled their screens. Then the ten viewed a picture of the three Razeur ships explode in rapid succession. Cheers came from the generals. Edward spoke again.

"Their flagship is heavily damaged but still there. Fire whatever pulse cannon is in range."

The ten generals nodded again and their last pulse canon just coming into range fired again and again. Seconds later the massive ship exploded. Edward sat at his computer in Alaska completely stunned. Against all the odds they had won a great victory. Their strategy worked. The Razeurs underestimated their strength and had paid the price for doing so.

Months later, Edward stood at the same podium in the United Nations as he had years earlier. But this time he made no security precautions. No one could claim the Razeurs did not exist. Many damaged cities and tens of millions of dead could attest to this fact. After accepting many accolades and awards, he answered one of many questions addressed to him. Edward never regarded their military victory as a total victory that others claimed.

"If we had not stopped the Razeurs when we did what would they have done and what will we do now to prevent them from returning?"

"According to the Knowldon, the Razeurs would have continued to attack until they encountered no resistance. Then they would have sent thousands of containers filled with viruses deadly to humans but harmless to Razeurs who more closely resemble our reptiles. The Razeurs would have waited several months until almost all humans died. If significant numbers survived in any area, they would have killed them with neutron bombs. Then they would have settled our planet and changed the climate to fit their preference for warm and humid conditions. The few humans that survived would have been made into slaves. That is what faced us and what will face us when the Razeurs return.

"When they do, they will have greater forces and different tactics. We will arm ourselves as best we can for the fight. We already have recovery efforts underway to salvage pieces of the Razeur ships in the hopes they will provide valuable technology we can use against the Razeurs. I understand four intact Razeur fighters and an additional ten damaged fighters have been recovered. This Razeur task force probably had as many as 1000 of these vessels. If they had launched, we might be looking at a very different battle outcome. I have also contacted the Knowldon asking for assistance. I will go to their world if necessary to make our case. I'm doubtful, however, of receiving any additional assistance from the Knowldon. In my brief conversation with them, they said that the Razeurs are blaming their defeat on the Knowldon and threatening war. Our best long-term strategy is to become a colony of the Knowldon, but under the present circumstances I don't know if this will be possible. The Knowldon will not want to aggravate the Razeurs anymore than they have already."

"At the end of the day, we have to work together and build our own defenses. Our survival is at stake. We have no room for petty arguments or conflicts. Thank you for all your help to date but we will need much more from you in the days and months ahead."

Edward wanted to end the conversation there but another question came.

"Edward when will the Razeurs return?"

"I have asked the Knowldon this question. The Razeurs are an empire that rules by force. They have interests spread throughout this part of the galaxy. They fear rebellion in the many colonies they rule, particularly so following our surprise victory. The Razeurs will slowly siphon off battleships from these areas and from their home world until they have a much larger armada with which to attack us. The Knowldon believe this will take at least a year in Earth time, perhaps a little longer."

A few weeks later, Edward stood in front of his picture window in Montana with Mary Ann at his side. After the Razeurs attacked Earth, the army abandoned their effort to undermine the house. He commented.

"Mary Ann many years ago I slept in a homeless camp in Chicago. Several residents lost their lives in a gang raid, but for whatever reason, I did not. I didn't really care whether I lived or died. Despite all my brilliance and talents, I felt like a useless empty shell. Then I met a beautiful young volunteer at the food pantry and my life changed. You saved me and because of the gifts given to me, I saved the world at least for now. When I journeyed to Knowldon, I thought I had lost you, but for reasons only known to you, you waited for me. I knew then that I would fight side by side with you until the end of my life and be a happy man doing so. Thank you for being you."

"Edward I have struggled to love you the way you deserve to be loved. This has been difficult for me. I have a long history of dating men then discarding them. But if my role in life is to keep you focused on what needs to be done to save this world, I now gladly embrace that role. I finally can say without reservation that I love you Edward and best of all for all the right reasons. Maybe one day we can spend the rest of our lives making music either here or on Knowldon. In the meantime, we will fight together to save the human race."

Edward and Mary Ann hugged passionately and watched the sun rise over the mountains.

INTERIM PERIOD

Without any governments hunting them as before, Mary Ann and Edward spent what little free time they had performing in small music venues, sometimes Mary Ann played with Edward and sometimes on her own. Edward even began to perform a little at the Chicago Symphony as a solo violinist. They finally had a little time to play music they always desired to play. Of course, they devoted most of their waking hours to coordinating worldwide defense preparations for the next Razeur invasion. The major countries in the world rebuilt their huge pulse canons, constructed new fighters based on Knowldon designs, and built new and improved self propelled nuclear mines as well. Unlike before, they did so with ever resource they had. They knew what would come for them. Also, with Edward's help, shields appeared on much of the world's key locations such as government buildings, science labs, and military facilities. The last Razeur attack killed tens of millions of people in some 30 cities worldwide. No one seemed to worry any longer which nation controlled these facilities. Edward worked on the science involved while Mary Ann worked on the communications side.

A year to the day after the failed Razeur attempt to destroy the world, Mary Ann approached Edward after a particularly long day for both of them. They sat by their penthouse window overlooking downtown Chicago. They had returned to their condo as soon as their government and other governments stopped pursuing them.

"Edward, be honest with me. What chance do we have to repel the Razeurs once again?"

"Despite world wide cooperation and plain hard work, not a very good one I am afraid. The Razeurs won't repeat the same mistakes as last time and will bring a much more powerful invasion force. Based on what they brought last time and what I anticipate they will bring, I have run hundreds of different simulations and in almost every one of them we lose. Of course, the longer they give us to prepare ourselves the better our options are, but for some of these simulations to show a possible victory we would need at least another year of preparation. I don't think the Razeurs will give us this long. Why do you ask all of a sudden?"

"For the best of reasons, I'm pregnant. Despite the odds, I still wanted to bring our child into the world. When we go, we need someone to carry on for us."

"Mary Ann despite what we face, I'm ecstatic over your news. I will fight all the harder to protect you and our child. Now I really know that you love me. I see a time when the three of us can play together." Edward said bringing Mary Ann into his arms. She replied with a smile.

"Yeah after he graduates from MIT."

"He can follow in my footsteps, a virtual chip off the old block." Edward laughed.

THE PILOTS

Jake Red from the time he could remember wanted to be one thing, an Air Force Fighter Pilot. He signed up for ROTC in college and went to flight school after joining the Air Force. From trainers to F-16's to F-15 to the F-22, Jake showed himself to be an excellent pilot. He had the right stuff. Jake for hard to explain reasons, always seemed to make the right move at the right time. No one had ever bested him in a dogfight. Like any master in his craft, Jake worked on his skills. He had few hobbies and no permanent relationships. He spent all his spare time working on new and unexpected moves on flight simulators. He lived to fly.

So to no one's surprise, Jake became a part of the new international fighter pilot group Avenging Angels. Equipped with Knowldon designed fighters, they trained daily to take on the Razeur fighters they would certainly encounter in the months or years ahead.

Jake approached the new Knowldon/Human fighter with the designation FK-99. The fighter looked a little like a F-22 but with its impulse engines, shields and pulse canons major differences could be noted everywhere. This handsome piece of hardware could fly to Mars in ten hours at fantastic speeds, climb vertically into space, turn at impossible angles and do so without any stress on the pilot. A dampening force applied to the pilot virtually eliminated the effects of gravity and centrifugal force. Travelling in the atmosphere at 20,000 miles per hour, the fighter could circle the earth in a little over an hour. A pilot did not use his hands and arms to control the fighter. Rather a direct link to the pilot's brain controlled all of the fighter's functions. All you had to do is think it. Then the fighter would respond.

Just before he reached his fighter, Jake ran into Jane Stone, his exact counterpart in the female gender. Jane possessed the same passion for flying and ability to fly as Jake. Like Jake her relationships never interfered with her desire to be the best possible pilot. She only became annoyed and hostile when men treated her as an attractive young brunette. She and Jake decided shortly after they met that they would become lovers but only to satisfy their sexual needs and wants. They both understood where both of their priorities lay. In fact, Jake told Jane that he could only date her and she responded in kind. Usually they treated each other as friendly rivals in public but today they reacted differently. Because they would meet the Razeur pilots for the first time today, both of them decided to spend their last night apart so they could concentrate on preparing for this day. Both Jake and Jane now regretted this decision. Jake spoke first.

"Jane I missed you in my bed. I've worked my whole life to fight this day but last night I couldn't sleep. One moment I thought of destroying many Razeur fighters the next I thought of never seeing you again. When I reached for you to comfort me, you weren't there. Somewhere along the way I fell in love with you. I don't now how or when it happened but it did. I never had time for romance before but now when I have the least time in my life, I am suddenly in the middle of it. Before we climb into those FK-99 cockpits, I want you to promise me if both of us survive this day, we will spend whatever time we have left together."

"Oh Jake I feel the same way. We are like part of each other. No other man would ever understand or tolerate me. Like you I thought of the dogfights to come one moment and the next I thought of making babies with you. I'm 28 years old and I have never had these thoughts before. Most girls start thinking this way as young teenagers. I've always liked men but they never fit into my world. I even thought about quitting the International Air Force and running away with you but of course I would never do that. If we don't fight the Razeurs with everything we have there will be no world for us. Just promise to return home tonight so we can be together."

"Jane I will but I must climb in my cockpit now before I decide not to do so. Just kiss and hug me a minute before I do."

"Technically, we don't have to climb in our airplanes until the alarm sounds. We could spend a little more time together."

"The Razeur fighter jets have been sighted heading toward Earth with their armada. The alarm can't be more than a few minutes away. I want to go over every single training instruction in my mind before I have to fly. You should do the same. If I am to return to you, I have to be at my very best. So do you."

"Okay Jake. I will do the same. Until we meet again my love."

With that remark, the two lovers spent almost five minutes hugging and kissing and then boarded their fighters. Ten minutes later the alarm sounded.

Ten long days later, Jake and Jane flew skyward in their scarred fighters, which had been patched together repeatedly. Only eight other planes flew next to them. Worldwide no more than fifty human planes remained. Hundreds of Razeur fighters suddenly appeared in the distance. Jake radioed Jane.

"Jane this is our end. We're good but not that good. I want you to know that the last nine nights have been the most wonderful of my life. I love you with all my heart. If there is life after death I will be there with you."

"Jake I feel the same way. I'm just sorry I couldn't have your child but because of our efforts other children will be born on Earth. I think we will have to be grateful for that. Goodbye my love. I'm going to take down as many Razeur fighters as I can before I go."

"So will I. Goodbye but hopefully not forever. Remember our tactic. We fly at maximum speed firing every weapon we have into the center of their formation. We start the firing sequence 10 seconds before the optimal firing range is reached to begin our firing before our opponents. Our fellow fighters will follow a similar attack on the exterior of the Razeur forces. We all have sophisticated ejection pods. When we reach a point where our flying can no longer make a difference, we will eject. I don't know how the ship's computer will time this ejection but at least we have a small chance of surviving."

"Yeah Jake. You know how this works. Despite the computer, our escape is unlikely in this battle to come. Even if we eject, the Razeurs will probably kill us. So let's concentrate on the task ahead. Come on handsome. Catch me if you can.'

Jake and Jane just as planned flew at maximum atmospheric speed into the center of the Razeur formation repeatedly firing every weapon they had. At first the speed and ferocity of their attack elicited only a limited response but by the time they flew through the enemy formation, both Jane and Jake felt the force of many pulses. Their shields visibly wavered. Still Jane and Jake accounted for 10 badly damaged or destroyed enemy fighters while the other 8 Knowldon/American fighters accounted for another 20 fighters. They had a great success but only three FK-99 had any fight left in them. Jake and Jane flew two of those three. Jake and Jane only had seconds to flee or turn once again on the enemy.

"Well Jane, I see no advantage in running now. They will easily catch and destroy us. Signal Rex to line up with us. Let's go down with our planes fighting, not running away." Jake said.

"Jake I feel the same. I'm turning for our second run. Rex is turning with us. We won't make it out other side but we will take more with us."

"Okay lined up Jane. Let's go. I love you."

The three FK-99 fighters commenced their second run taking out three additional Razeur fighters but as Jane said, with over 60 Razeur fighters firing at them, the three FK-99 fighters blew into a thousand pieces before they completed their run. Unfortunately other FK-99 fighters did not have as much success as Jane and Jake did in their battle. At the end of the day with some help from the Razeur main ships, the FK-99 fighters only destroyed slightly more Razeur fighters than the Razeurs did FK-99's.

THE FINAL CONFLICT

Edward sat at his computer in the same way he had a year and a half earlier. The Alaska spring produced some moderating temperatures but snow still covered the forests and the mountains. A very pregnant Mary Ann walked in and out of his study. The same ten military men as before joined the call with him. Moments later, three Omar Class and six Kamar Class battleships dropped out of hyperspace between the orbits of Mars and Earth, but this time much closer to Mars than Earth. A thousand cloaked fusion mines headed for the massive ships. Only one hundred of these mines lay near enough to reach the vessels in the next several hours. The remainder would continue to attack the Razeur ships as they headed to Earth.

Unlike before, the Razeur vessels did not immediately form a wedge and head for Earth. Rather, they launched all their 3000 fighters. The fighters immediately began to scan for the cloaked mines even though First Admiral Sun did not expect to encounter them this far from Earth. He would not make the same mistakes his long time friend and colleague Admiral Blaze made. His fighters would attack until the Earth became defenseless. One of his fighters and his own Battleship Annihilation picked up the cloaked mines at the same time. In a great surprise, the mines hurled toward them at the very high rate of speed, 1% of the speed of light. More mines quickly came into view. The fighter immediately fired on the first mine but the moment the pulse canon struck the mine, the nuclear portion of the mine exploded with its energy turned toward the Annihilator. Other mines as the fighters and battleships identified them also exploded with their fusion energy turned toward one of the Razeur ships. The barrage seemed to go on forever.

Then in the confusion of the battle, the four captured Razeur fighters slipped into the conflict obscured by a number of self-propelled mines. Earth scientists led by Edward, programmed the fighters to enter the nearest Razeur ship with hydrogen bombs and detonate the moment they penetrated the shield. No one piloted these ships. The first fighter penetrated the shield of one of the Omar class vessels, the Oblivion, and exploded. As soon as it did, all the Razeur vessels reprogramed their shields. When they did, the remaining three fighters could no longer gain access through any of the shields and fell to overwhelming fire from the Razeur vessels. While the first fighter's explosion should have destroyed the Oblivion, the new Omar Class vessel had two shields in the launch area. When the Razeur fighter penetrated the first shield, the remaining shield immediately activated when the Razeur fighter failed to enter the special entry code for the Oblivion. Nonetheless, the subsequent explosion damaged both the primary and secondary Oblivion's shields making them more susceptible to subsequent attacks.

Admiral Sun calmly ordered his armada to proceed toward Earth. Although all his ships showed some damage and twenty eight fighters in the path of the fusion weapons exploded, Admiral Sun knew that at some point the enemy's cloaked fusion mines would be exhausted. The damage to the Oblivion landing bay shields also provided some concern but fortunately the stolen fighters targeted the Omar Class as opposed to the Kamar Class ships, which did not have a secondary shield. Also, unlike Admiral Blaze's previous battle, the mines in this attack detonated farther away from his ships and exploded one at a time creating far less damage to the Razeur ships. Still, two of his Kamar Class ships suffered enough damage to be taken out of the fight and the remainder of his ships showed signs of damage in addition to what the Oblivion suffered. His own Annihilator, after six mines struck the launch area, could no longer launch or land any fighters, but his repair crews told Sun that they could repair the launch bays in about 24 Earth hours. In a clever move, the Earthlings concentrated their attacks on this area. In fact, only his sister ship Oblivion could land or launch any vessels and with weakened shields might not be able to do this much longer. The damaged fighters that could still function headed there for repairs.

By the time the Razeur fleet reached Earth orbit several days later, two more Kamar Class ships had been disabled and the Oblivion too with its weakened shields had lost its launch and landing capability, but the Annihilator regained its launch capability. 800 fighters, stuck on the Oblivion no longer participated in the battle. Admiral Sun with 2200 fighters remaining did not worry about the lost fighters, he still had more than enough. Also eventually most of these 800 fighters would return to the battle. He did worry about the loss of his four Kamar Class ships. While their crews worked furiously on restoring the ships to full operation, none would be repaired in enough time to join the battle at least at the beginning. Admiral Sun considered delaying the attack to allow those ships to rejoin the fight but he could not afford to lose the attack advantage he now had. Pausing in the middle of a battle also gave time to the enemy to regroup and reposition its forces.

As he prepared to once again fire on all the Earth's military facilities and major cities, over one hundred mines attacked his fleet at the same time. He lost another two hundred fighters in the attack and one Kamar Class ship became disabled but finally Earth's fusion mines seemed to have been exhausted. No sooner had he concluded this fight, when 10 massive pulse canons on Earth opened on his ships. Admiral Sun expecting this attack targeted all his remaining ship's guns on the pulse canons and fired them repeatedly until they finally fell silent. The Earth pulse canons, however, cost the admiral his final Kamar Class ship when it lost all power and caused further damage to his other ships including his own. Now down to 1900 fighters and three Omar Class ships with a total of 45 operational pulse guns, Admiral Sun could finally begin his bombardment of Earth.

As the bombardment began, 800 Earth based fighters, copies of the latest Knowldon design, began to engage Admiral Sun's fighters. Roughly equal to the Razeur fighters, the spectacular dogfights resulted in only slightly greater losses for the Razeur forces. After several long hours, the last of the Earth fighters exploded but Admiral Sun's fighter force now had been reduced to 1059 active fighters. In those hours, however, Admiral Sun damaged many Earth cities and destroyed many Earth military facilities. Unlike last time, some of the cities and military facilities had shields. Rather than waste time with these targets, Sun merely switched to undefended cities and military facilities. When he laid waste to all these facilities, he turned his attack toward the better-defended ones.

Finally, once again to Sun's surprise, satellite based pulse canons began to fire on his ships along with another Earth based pulse canon just coming into range. They concentrated their fire on the Oblivion. The formidable ship finally lost power and lay suspended in space. Admiral Sun called the Captain who said he temporarily lost power but would return power in a short time. When he did, he would immediately contact his admiral. His weakened shields in the landing bay area proved to be too good a target for the enemy. Slowly, Admiral Sun destroyed all his new targets, but lost another hundred fighters. Also, his two operational Omar Class ships now had only 28 working pulse canons between the two of them but without significant enemy fighting resources left, Admiral Sun felt he had more than enough of a fighting force left to win the war. Also, the admiral expected some of his Kamar Class damaged ships to return to the fight soon. As a result, the Admiral calmly put out a system wide call to drop the virus cylinders. Over one thousand left the Razeur ships toward Earth. Most of the remaining fighters accompanied the canisters on their journey to Earth. Yet at this moment, the final massive pulse cannon came in range. Instead of firing on the Razeur vessels, the pulse canon started eliminating the canisters and the fighters that accompanied them. Admiral Sun concentrated his twenty-eight operational guns on the pulse canon. Finally, the Earth gun exploded but not before over 500 canisters had been destroyed along with another 300 fighters. Admiral Sun sighed. The remaining canisters would probably still do the job but it would take longer. Also thousands of primitive chemical based jets attacked the canisters. Hundreds of additional canisters exploded but his superior fighters made short work of the primitive jets. With only some ground-based resources remaining, The Earthlings destroyed more canisters but in the end over 150 reached the ground and opened.

Admiral Sun left his command seat for the first time in days and went to eat some living food. The dispersal of the viruses had not gone well but the virus would spread over time from the opened containers. Also, the admiral would use neutron bombs to supplement the lost canisters. He had hundreds at his disposal. Already his remaining Razeur fighters were being equipped with the devices. The human population would eventually be reduced to almost zero. His remaining guns punished the human cities. Effective human resistance finally came to an end. All his ships despite many suffering heavy damage could eventually be repaired and returned to the fight with most of their weapons still operational. The price had been very high but the objective had been achieved. Many Razeur warriors would receive the military funerals they had earned. Admiral Sun would make sure the Earthlings paid dearly for the Razeurs they killed. He would not leave a single living human on this world. Yet despite his need for revenge he grudgingly acknowledged that the humans fought bravely. Perhaps a few humans could be left alive.

As Admiral Sun finished his meal, a squirming mammal that looked like an Earth mouse, and sipped some water, his chief aide Captain Fire came running up to him.

"Admiral, come to the bridge quickly. A Knowlton Armada has dropped out of hyperspace near Earth. They are launching almost 2000 fighters and opening fire on our ships. Their guns are much more powerful than the ones we have experienced elsewhere. Our other Omar Class ship the Bomb has sustained heavy damage. Like the Oblivion, it is out of operation. The . . ."

In the next moment, Admiral Sun flew through the air into the wall. In pain, he left his seat and wandered his bridge rallying his other officers to the fight. As he and his team brought systems on line, Admiral Sun realized that a new war erupted between the Knowldon and Razeur empires. Yet as Admiral Sun fantasized about his role in this new war another powerful Knowldon pulse struck his ship. A brilliant sun enveloped and devoured him.

Throughout the long battle, Edward stayed at his computer offering what little advice he could to the ten generals and admirals making the military decisions. After the first hour, they all knew that in the end Earth would lose. The Razeurs had brought too much firepower for them to counter. Yet they bravely fought on for ten long days. When almost all of their guns, planes and mines had been silenced, Edward rose from his computer and sought Mary Ann.

"Mary Ann we've put up a great fight, destroyed much of the enemy's weapons but the Razeurs brought two much firepower for us to win. We have nothing left to fight them. They are releasing the deadly virus canisters and I expect they will soon start to deploy neutron bombs to kill those of us not killed by the virus. Our time on this Earth grows short. We will have to go to the Knowlton transport site before this no longer becomes an option."

"Okay I guess we have no choice. I will get ready, but I feel cowardly abandoning Earth to its fate."

"I feel the same way, but as you have said we have no other options."

As Edward turned toward the area where a destroyed pulse canon now lay in ruins, he saw a virus canister float slowly toward the Earth. Reacting with lightning speed, he activated several pulse canons he installed in his house following the first war with the Razeurs. Just before the canister hit the ground, Edward fired all his pulse canons at it. The canister exploded seconds later. Unfortunately, Edward's actions triggered a response from a nearby Razeur fighter. Its pulse canons hit his home's shields with tremendous force. Edward returned fire from his pulse canons but the fighter's shields blocked most of his fire. The Razeur fighter banked and came back for a second attack. Edward fired again as did the Razeur fighter. The shields protecting his house began to fluctuate, but he did not detect much fluctuation in the fighter's shields. The Razeur fighter would win this exchange. As a warship, the

Razeur fighter had stronger shields and pulse canons. His home and he and Mary Ann inside of it would be obliterated.

At just this moment, a strong voice came over their speaker system.

"I can see a Razeur fighter is creating problems for you. I'm targeting it now. There this should eliminate the threat."

Seconds later a powerful pulse came from space and struck the fighter. The fighter exploded in a large fireball.

"If you haven't guessed this is Trill, your old friend from Knowldon. I'm a Captain in the Knowldon Armada that has arrived in your system and engaged the Razeurs. There will be no need for you to leave Earth. We will need you here. Unlike most of our battles with the Razeurs, this battle is not much of a fight. You've damaged their Armada so badly they have no chance against us. We will eliminate all their ships and send fighters to destroy the fighters they have remaining. We will have to work quickly before some Razeur ships escape into hyperspace. With your permission we will dispatch our medical personnel to contain and destroy the viruses that have been deployed. We will also help your scientist's develop vaccines for those at risk of exposure and anti-virals that should cure some of those already infected. Many Earthlings will die from the viruses but if we act quickly most humans can be saved. While these sentient lives are irreplaceable, you will survive as a race. Of course, the damage the Razeurs have inflicted on your cities is great. We estimate as a result of the two attacks more than one and a half billion humans have died or will die in the near future. Yet your cities can be rebuilt and repaired and your population can be restored. Finally, you will need a major clean up operation in the space surrounding Earth. Radioactive debris from your exploding mines and the Razeur fighters and ships will have to be collected and sent to the sun for destruction. Otherwise, your satellite systems won't work well. You will suffer worldwide communication disruptions damaging to your planet. Despite all this loss, we are prepared to offer you our technical assistance in addressing these problems. Also, I am happy to report that our high council is prepared to offer you admittance to our empire. We will request that you be the liaison between the Empire and Earth. Once you join us we can help you rebuild your military and defend you against any future Razeur attacks. Believe it or not, the Razeurs will come again with an even greater force. They do not accept defeat."

"Why would you do this Trill? You and your government repeatedly told me that you did not want to become involved.'

"Your brave and resourceful defense of your world has changed the entire dynamic in the Razeur colonies. They are in open revolt as a result of your successes. The resources they have deployed here and their losses have made them much less able to contain these revolts. Their empire after thousands of years is collapsing. We couldn't strategically afford to let you lose. Also, we stole the latest pulse canon design they are using on their new Omar class ships and improved upon it. While you stayed on our home world you actually helped me and other scientists make those improvements. I must say we were very surprised by the incredible creative quotient you have, which we assume you share with your human brothers and sisters. This means your race may be very helpful in the Razeur war we must fight now. In any case, many of our military leaders wanted to test the effectiveness of these new weapons you helped develop in a combat situation. We are doing just that with great success today.

"Even so the council refused to authorize the deployment of this armada until they were reminded of the music. No more Earthlings no more of their divine music. When the council sampled public opinion, they found overwhelming public support to save you and your music. The council changed its mind and we came as a result. You made our job easy. On your own, you almost defeated a sizable Razeur Armada after defeating a smaller one. You truly are, despite being thousands of years behind us in technology, an impressive people."

"Trill my old friend, thank you for believing in me and us and thank you for providing some of your advanced technologies with which to fight the Razeurs. I will do whatever I can to convince my fellow humans to join your confederation of planets as a colony. This will not be an easy task. Our losses are staggering. The world will be in shock and looking for someone to blame. But in the end they will see the wisdom of joining you."

"Thank you. I hope to see you soon after we have eliminated the Razeur Armada. Our new pulse canons are working very well indeed. Already five of their Kamar Class and two of their Omar Class vessels have exploded. Their remaining Omar Class and Kamar Class vessels will soon be gone as well. Our losses are minimal. The Razeurs will of course threaten war with us, but with their revolts and losses here they can no longer wage a successful war on us. To the contrary, we are considering a major attack on the Razeurs to eliminate them as a threat. We will see. Anyway, I hope we can work together to rebuild your world."

When the transmission ended, Edward turned to Mary Ann and said.

"As it should be music literally saved our world."

"Yes it did and now we need to get back to making it together and laying the ground work for our trio even though our son Michael won't be born for a few weeks."

"Ha instead of a rattle he will have a miniature violin. You can't start them too early." Edward laughed.

EPILOGUE

Edward with a light radiation suit walked solemnly through the strange landscape before him. In the middle of the Congo in what should have been one of the densest and most verdant places on the planet, Edward saw nothing but devastation. Everything within a 50-mile radius died when a Razeur neutron bomb exploded here. Large earthmovers had already removed the thousands of dead animals including humans littered everywhere, but the black and rotting plants and trees remained. When everything finally left here, the earth itself would look more like the moon than the jungle it should be. Some living things had returned, an occasional plant sent a shoot skyward, but death would be the theme of this area for many years to come. A hundred sites like this dotted the world. At first the bombs fell on cities not protected by shields but at the very end, the Razeurs just dumped the bombs where they could before the Knowldon destroyed them. Along with the 70 virus containers that opened in the world, these bombs and the laser pulse blasts killed an estimated 1.7 billion people and countless other animals, leaving the earth with only 6 billion people. The virus spread so rapidly that only a last minute joint effort with the Knowldon managed to stop the deadly epidemic before it destroyed the entire human race.

As the world's liaison to the Knowldon, Edward occupied one of the most important posts in this new Earth. This is why he had to come to one of these sites to feel the enormity of the tragedy that had befallen Earth. Tears already flowed onto his cheeks. What he witnesses here was pure evil, the final solution alien style. With newfound purpose,

Edward swore that he would do whatever it took to stop this tragedy from recurring. If the Razeurs returned, they would receive a welcome unlike their last ones. He would destroy these monsters even if it cost him his life to do so.